DOGLESS IN METCHOSIN

DOGLESS IN METCHOSIN

TOM HENRY

HARBOUR

Harbour Publishing
P.O. Box 219
Madeira Park, BC Canada V0N 2H0

Cover and inside illustrations by Greta Guzek
Cover design by Roger Handling, Terra Firma Design
Page design and composition by Lionel Trudel, Aspect Design
Author photo by Lorna Jackson
Printed and bound in Canada

Stories in this collection appeared, in somewhat different form, on
CBC Radio. "Making Hay" was first published in the *Vancouver Sun*.

Excerpt from *Measure of the Year* by Roderick Haig-Brown,
© 1950, published by Douglas & McIntyre Ltd. Reprinted by permission.

Canadian Cataloguing in Publication Data

Henry, Tom, 1961 -
Dogless in Metchosin

ISBN 1-55017-130-5

1. Country life—British Columbia—Metchosin—Anecdotes. 2. Country life—
British Columbia—Metchosin—Humor. 3. Metchosin (B.C.)—Social life and
customs—Anecdotes. 4. Metchosin (B.C.)—Social life and customs—Humor. 5.
Canadian wit and humor (English) I. Title.
PS8565.E44D6 1995   C818'.5402   C95-910735-5
PR9199.3.H46D6 1995

To Mom and Dad

Contents

SUMMER

ESTATE CARS

Every morning at about seven o'clock, my family wakes to the sound of the landlord's Suzuki 4x4 zooming up his long driveway to get the newspaper. Unmuffled and underpowered, it makes the same sounds as my three-year-old, Lily, guiding her toy dump truck through dishes on the counter. Vroom! Vroom, vroom! Vrooomm! *Vrooooooommmmmmm!* If the wind isn't blowing too hard I can keep my head on the pillow and follow the 4x4's progress to the top of the drive, half a mile away.

The Suzuki is the landlord's estate car. "Estate car" is the high-handed phrase people in this part of southern Vancouver Island use to describe the unlicensed, uninsured and generally dilapidated cars and trucks they need for errands on their property: fetching the newspaper, hauling hay to the livestock or dragging the power washer back from the shop. Sometimes you'll see these vehicles dashing illegally along a country back road. Property owners have at least one, and they are as much a part of the landscape as satellite dishes, forty-five-gallon fuel drums and claw bathtub watering troughs.

Spotting an estate car is easy, if you know what to look for. Because they often undergo fairly radical changes—either unintentionally through run-ins with hemlock stumps, or intentionally at the hands of owners with oxygen/acetylene torches—you can't identify them by make and model. It's far better to concentrate on smoke and noise.

Smoke is as common to estate cars as fleas and bad breath are to dogs. This is because their engines are worn and out of tune. The smoke isn't always your #1 Pennzoil either, as owners tend to dump whatever goop is on hand into the engine. Like bar oil for the chain saw. That comes out of an old engine as a sour pink mist. Run into a nasty haze on a country road and there's a good chance an estate car is nearby.

As for noise, odds are that you'll hear an estate car before you see it. Not only is it impossible to keep a muffler on a vehicle that's in regular contact with boulders, ditches and chunks of wood, but the throaty brap that comes out of a straight pipe lets deer know something's coming as well.

The surest way to tell the difference between estate cars and regular vehicles is to look at the driver's face. If the driver looks like he just goofed the morning away eating raisin pie, drinking coffee and talking with friends about hunting moose in the Chilcotin, then he's in an estate car. If he looks as if he *wished* he had goofed the morning away doing all those things, instead of diligently paying bills in town, then he's in a regular vehicle.

My landlord is a good example of what driving an estate car can do to a person. When Dave shows up in his main vehicle, a swanky 1993 red Chev 1-ton with duals, he's all business. The engine stays running; he doesn't leave the cab. "Any more trouble with the

Dixon seal on that water pump? Good. Well, if you notice the pressure climbing over 120 psi switch to the bypass and hit number two, just like I showed you. Gotta go." Then he drives off too slowly, like he's trying to figure out if that big leafy plant we've got in the vegetable garden is legal or not.

Dave in the Suzuki is a person transformed. The first thing he does after roaring down the driveway is shut the engine off. (Actually it stalls.) Then he gets out, slams the driver's door twice, smiles, and wanders around the passenger side and gets down on all fours, peering intently. "Loose wheel bearing," he says, reaching an arm obscenely far up into a wheel well. "Pass me the vicegrips, will you?"

There's a pair of vicegrips under the Suzuki's passenger seat, and I've got so I can lay my hand on them without looking. What exactly Dave does with them I don't know, but he usually taps a bit, tries to tighten something, slips, makes a face and says he'll get to it tomorrow. Then he gets up, wipes his hands on his pants and asks if there's any tea.

Two hours and five cups later, having rearranged the province's tree farm system and played a marathon game of peek-a-boo with Lily, he leaves with a wave and a toot. If it's after dark by this time, I'll stay at the open door and listen, to make sure he gets home all right.

THIS CABIN

T he place that Lorna, Lily and I have called home for the last two years is a cedar-shingled cabin at the head of a small bay in Metchosin. The cabin is L-shaped, with kitchen to the west, two bedrooms to the east, and a rectangular living room in the middle.

The living room is the oldest part of the structure. It dates to the turn of the century, maybe earlier. Back then it was a single-room shack. A Japanese boatbuilder lived in it. The landlord found Japanese newspaper insulating the walls while he was renovating a few years ago. I think of that boatbuilder whenever Lily overturns a glass of juice. The floor slopes, so the juice sloshes into one corner, making for easy cleanup. Wiping, I wonder: was the floor sloped then? Did the Japanese boatbuilder have kids? What sloshed across these dark fir floors in those days?

Rent as many cabins as I have over the years, and it's impossible to think of them as your home only. There are so many echoes of former tenants in places like this—homemade gate locks, exotic perennials, strychnine and mousetraps in the attic—that it seems you're yet another generation in an old, old family.

Echo: A driftwood garden box on the side of the cabin. Several years ago, a shrubby type of guy rented the place and grew pot. He scoped out the location, then built the soil up with manure and seaweed, all contained in nicely built boxes. We don't use the same garden for marijuana, but it makes for excellent beefsteak tomato and tobacco crops.

Echo: Westerly winds push logs and junk from the Pacific into the Juan de Fuca Strait, then local currents eddy the junk from the strait into our bay. On nights with a heavy westerly, loose logs thunk and bonk against the steel floats in the bay, and I'm reminded of a man named Gary.

Gary used to live here. He also worked for a log booming company that had an operation in the bay. At lunch, instead of having cold sandwiches with the rest of the crew, Gary hopped a log and poled it casually back to this cabin, and made himself a hot lunch. When he was done, he'd pole back out to the lunch float. Gary had one particular log for this, which came to be known as Gary's log. The thunk of Gary's log hitting the float signalled the rest of the crew it was time to get back to work.

My landlord told me about Gary and his log soon after we moved in here—like it was something I should know, along with the idiosyncrasies of the water pump and the mail delivery. That, in turn, told me things were going to be just fine between Dave and me. Anyone who admires the idea of poling home on a log for lunch has to be OK.

Echo: Every cabin has to have one sad story, and the sad story of this cabin is about Mike. I won't forget this one, because Dave told me about it after I mentioned my intentions of living by my wits, close enough to the land that my family has at least a hint of self-sufficiency.

Mike had a dream too. He was a geologist from Alberta. He and a friend moved here just after they got out of school. This is twenty, twenty-five years ago. The friend got a job right away, but Mike didn't have the luck. After some time looking, he started doing odd jobs at the docks. This led to contact with commercial fishermen, and Mike was offered a job on a troller. As it turned out, the season set records. Mike made fifteen thousand dollars in a few months. More important, he fell in love with fishing. That winter, Mike sat in this cabin reading, studying, talking with old-timers. Learned everything he could. Next season, he bought a troller. It was a junker, but he worked it hard and made money. In several years he made enough to build his own boat. It was to be the ultimate. A combination troller-sailer. Forty-eight feet. Lines like a bullet. He had it designed, and he arranged shipyard space. Everything was ready to go.

Then the plan collapsed. The shipyard had double-booked. The next season was crappy. Mike lost his dream boat, his regular boat, then his shirt. Finally, he gave Dave notice and took off—leaving this cabin to fill with mice, waiting for the next dreamer to move in.

CHILD LABOUR
LAWS

*I*t takes three cords of wood to heat our cabin for the winter. Lily and I put this wood up June and July, sawing and stacking several armfuls each morning. I use a thirty-six-inch crosscut saw; Lily stands atop the hemlock chopping block and cheers. "Come on, saw!" she says, whenever the blade binds. "Come on. Come *on!*"

I like working with Lily. She knows when it's time to break for bread and jam, which has to be fifty percent of woodcutting. Fresh bread smeared with an inch of yellow plum jam.

Lily also keeps me from working at any one job too long. Each morning we manage to put in a half hour cutting wood before she gets bored and starts winging rocks at the chickens. Then we head to the garden, then up to the neighbour's to rake her lawn, then back down to gunge out the chicken coop, and so on and so on from job to job until it's time for lunch.

This has been going on for two years. The result is that our yard is awash in uncut logs and unfinished fences. Last time I counted, there were at least fifteen big projects that needed doing around here. There may be more, but Lily didn't let me finish tallying them all.

At one time in my life this would have driven me crazy. I used to like putting my head down and doing a job all at once. Not any more. I like the choices implicit in chaos. Having lots of projects means there's always something to move on to when Lily gets bored; it means she doesn't have time to put crayons in a hot oven, or bugger off down a country lane.

Working with a kid also lets you see the world from a different point of view. People, like airliners, operate at fixed elevations. For me, it's the 5'6" to 6'6" zone. Above and below that I don't notice much. Lily, on the other hand, hugs the ground. Nothing in the zero-to-three-foot category escapes her eye. Consequently we didn't have a single slug make it to the romaine lettuce this summer. And if it wasn't for Lily, I would never have found the rat hole by the chimney.

But the best part of working with a kid is the company. Not only are children fun themselves—jumping up and down when they see the moon and yelling at caterpillars and all that stuff—but so are their imaginary buddies.

With Lily, most of these characters appear when we walk up the lane to check the mail. I pull her plastic wagon and load it with fallen branches. When the wagon gets really full, I make Lily pull too. Sometimes she finds this tedious and conjures up all sorts of friends to help. At various times in the last six months, we've been assisted by a pair of dinosaurs, Franklin the Turtle, a baby and a bunch of aunts and uncles I've never heard of, but who Lily knows intimately.

A few weeks ago, I dragged a large windfall out of the bush

and heaved it onto the lane. Lily screamed, "Not there! *Not there!*" My first thought was that a chunk had shot off and hit her. But after she calmed down, I discovered I'd flattened a whole troupe of imaginary pals.

All I could do was apologize, and promise that as soon as we got home I'd fix three pieces of fresh bread slathered in yellow plum jam—one for her, one for me, and one for her buddies.

IN DEFENCE

OF CHICKENS

The centre of our home economy is our flock of chickens. We have eight, all hens. They are ISA Browns, a poultry version of the Chrysler K car: moderate size, even temperament, nice wattle, not prone to getting egg-bound. Each of our chickens produces one egg per day, day in day out, no matter what the circumstances. This is remarkable, because circumstances around here are rarely conducive to peaceful egg laying. Too many hawks and dogs. A hawk tried taking one of the hens the other day. I came down the drive and heard a terrified *Bock! Bock! Bock!*—that being the sound chickens make when they are being torn apart and eaten. The hawk, a Cooper's, was atop the hen, as if mating. I hollered and the hawk took off with a defiant squawk. The hen, minus a pillowful of feathers, stumbled under the coop. I figured: "So much for that hen, we'll be down to seven eggs a day."

Next day, eight eggs.

The same thing happened when the landlord's idiot black lab slipped off its chain and got at the chickens. I was on the phone, long distance, when I heard *Bock! Bock! Bock!* I zoomed out in time to see a hen struggle from the dog's mouth and flop under a car. Dave arrived to re-educate the dog with an axe handle, and I gave the chicken up for soup stock.

Next day, eight eggs.

I like chickens. I like them so much I feel compelled to formally come to their defence, and dispel a few mistaken notions.

First, chickens are not chicken. A chicken is a social animal that, given the chance, would live with people inside the home, snoozing by the woodstove and watching TV. This is exactly what our chickens did when we first got them last summer. At that time I had some hippie-type notion about letting the flock freely scratch around our yard, picking slugs and worms. And they did—for three days. Then they discovered the windows to the house and took to perching on the ledges, watching us eat dinner, tapping inquisitively at the glass. Next, they took to dashing into the house whenever we opened the doors. Within two weeks of getting our flock, we were reluctant to open a door or window, and it occurred to me that the wrong species was cooped up.

Friends were over from Vancouver one afternoon and, after having coffee while the kids watched too many videos, we decided to go for a walk. In the confusion of leaving, the back door was left ajar. The chickens toured the house, clockwise. They stopped in front of the TV, scratched at the carpet, paused by the woodstove, then left. By the time we returned, they were outside again. I was able to reconstruct their trespass from the evidence, which took a roll of paper towel to remove.

After this, I decided to confine the chickens. So much for the live-and-let-live hippie lifestyle.

This brings me to another point about chickens. They are not stupid. Especially in a flock. The more chickens you have, the greater their collective intelligence. It's as if they hook up in series, like batteries in a logging truck, to achieve a voltage greater than any individual. This is the absolute opposite of humans, who get stupider and stupider as they gather—the ultimate proof being multinational corporations, unions, parliamentary committees, etc.

I took the opportunity of my friends' visit to erect a fence around the chicken coop. Four feet high, spiked to cedar fence posts. It took three of us a morning. We put the chickens in at quarter to twelve. Half an hour later, over lunch, one of my guests pointed at the window: Look. There were two chickens, perched on the ledge, bobbing their heads at us, gently ting-tinging at the pane.

To abbreviate what took place over the next eighteen hours, suffice it to say our collective brains weren't functioning well. If the chickens were getting over a four-foot fence, we thought, then we'll make the fence five feet high. So we strung wire at five feet, then six, six and a half, then seven. Each time, the chickens flew over.

How long this would have gone on had Dave not showed up, I don't know. But the next morning, as my friends and I were preparing to do battle with the flock again, we heard the telltale vroom of the Suzuki approaching. Dave has had chickens before and is definitely not the hippie type. He took one look at our soaring fence, then at the chickens milling and scratching around the yard, and said: "Why don't you clip their wings?"

It was a painfully clear thought, and it sunk in like a dog's tooth. Just a few inches of feather off the wing tips and they can't get airborne.

Dave was aghast. "You mean, you didn't think about clipping their wings?" he said.

"Well, no," I said, grasping for any excuse. "It never occurred to me. There were … three of us. You know how people are when they get together."

We clipped the chicken's wings that afternoon; they haven't been off the ground since. Now our doors are open, our carpets are unsoiled and—behold—we get eight eggs, day after day.

HETTI EDBURG'S

BEE

T his morning I received a phone call from the president of the
local community organization. She said there was a work bee
coming up in a couple of weeks, and since my family was new to the
area—i.e., we'd been here less than a decade—she thought we might
want to come out and meet some neighbours. I said it was a very nice
offer, but drat the luck of pigs, that was the weekend my cousin
Midge was getting married. Couldn't miss that. I thanked her again,
and said bye.

Truth is, there's probably no worse way of making friends
than getting into a community work bee. My parents discovered this
years ago when we moved to a farm in Groundbirch, in the Peace
River country of BC. We'd been there about six months when the
president of the local community association, a woman named Hetti
Edburg, drove up in a baby-blue Buick and invited us to the annual

spring tidy-up of the community cemetery. Hetti, a big and forceful woman, framed the invitation in such a way as to make it impossible to say no without slighting the memory of her late husband, Johan Edburg, who was buried in the cemetery along with other big players in the area's history.

So my parents accepted the invitation.

Up to this point, the only community-type thing they'd done was attend a school board meeting. That hadn't worked out so well because halfway through the meeting, my dad, who has a keen eye, rose and pointed out that the figures on a pie chart of the board's budget added up to 106%. Red-faced, the board members huddled for a few minutes, then came up with the typical school board answer: Mr. Henry was out of order. Should the "new resident," as they put it, like to discuss matters further, he was welcome to drive thirty-five miles into Dawson Creek and meet with the officials, available Friday mornings, ten o'clock to ten-fifteen.

My parents and I arrived at the cemetery, which was really the size of a small field, and went to work. The schedule, as set and posted by Hetti, was to rake the edges of the grounds, have lunch, then trim and mow around the actual graves.

Everything went fine—until lunch. My dad never went anywhere without a case of Silver Spring beer, and, in deference to the occasion, had brought two cases. This proved especially popular with the men, who crowded around our picnic blanket guzzling beer and heaping their plates with Mom's potato salad.

It wasn't so popular with Hetti, whose contribution to the day was a thick, goopy drink made from Osterized watermelon and cantaloupe, that (she claimed) "made you feel good all over." Buckets of the stuff sat unquaffed.

After lunch, things went from bad to worse. Unfamiliar with the effects of beer at midday, several of the men lay down on the spot and snoozed. Meanwhile others, including Dad, fired up the lawn mowers and attacked the long grass with harvest season vigour. Around they went, back and forth, sweating and grunting. The lot was just about clean when Dad, attempting a shortcut, ran into a grave. There was an awful whang, followed by a long and lengthy cuss from Dad. Then a cry of "Oh, Johan" from Hetti. Dad had hit Johan's grave.

The grave was intact. But Hetti and the rest of the community big shots never forgave my family for what went on that day. Five years later, when failed crops forced us to leave the farm, they all pitched in and gave us the ugliest clock imaginable. Hetti presented it herself. "Hang it where I can see it when I come to visit," she told Dad. Of course she's never been down to visit, but that clock still hangs over my parents' kitchen sink, a bad taste testimony to the hazards of the community work bee.

TWO ANGRY TAILLIGHTS

Eating pizza-joint pizza may not sound like the most rural of habits, but if you ate as much homemade cabbage soup or as many homemade carrot/zucchini/squash muffins as we do, you'd crave salt and animal fat too.

Where I live—at the end of a lane, off a side road, off a secondary road—it's not possible to get a hot feta-and-onion pizza delivered to our door. It's possible to get a hot one delivered accidentally to a neighbouring farmer's door, and it's possible to get a tepid one delivered to our door, but a hot one to this cabin? No.

I know this because I've tried many times to get hot pizza delivered, and I've always met with failure. The fifteen miles between my house and the nearest pizza joint is just too much for a kid in a Corolla to handle. So what I've taken to doing is meeting the kid halfway, which around here puts you right at the wooden bench.

The wooden bench is a landmark of sorts. Sixteen feet long and capped with a hand-split cedar shake roof, it sits under a maple at the west end of what is optimistically referred to as downtown: elementary school, two gas stations, general store, café, pottery shop and sagging community hall. Everyone knows where the bench is; it's a depot for kids, parcels, couriers and farm workers—as well as pizzas.

Picking slivers out of a wooden bench may not sound like an ideal way to pass the time while waiting for pizza, but I've come to enjoy it. I get to hear how the community is doing.

Normally I drive through town at 30 mph, watching for dogs and listening to radio reports on the latest east coast cod disaster. On the bench, I get to listen to the real news. Five o'clock and Hawthornewaite's already idling down his Kenworth? Log prices must be off. Five-fifteen and the gas jockeys have time to skiff a fris-bee around? Hmmm. Gas prices must be even more out of line than usual. Squeal of three air wrenches from the garage down the road? Maybe Frank and Mandy have finally put those radials on sale.

Another reason I like waiting at the bench is watching the daily traffic jam. Or our version of a daily traffic jam—this is one you won't hear newscasters talking about. There are two types of people on or near the roads around here after five p.m.: stressed-out assistant deputy ministers and surly building contractors. The assistant deputy ministers are hurtling home in BMWs, the building con-tractors are standing halfway on the road, leaning on piles of twenty-foot-long 2x12s sticking out of their pickups. The two usually meet in a terrible clash at the blind corner in front of the store at about 5:35—earlier on Fridays. Brakes squeal, tires chatter and dogs and bystanders scatter. The contractors hoist tanned and dirty middle fin-gers; the assistant deputy ministers toot their horns. Then, in the time it takes to place a finger against one nostril and blow, the thing is over. The BMWs are off in a hum of over-revved engine, the dogs come out from under parked cars and all there is to do is settle back and wait.

Perched on the bench, waiting, there is time to gossip with passers-by or neighbours waiting for pizza. Gossip is typically a leisurely affair, conducted from the kitchen with the phone in the crick of your neck and your hands in beet juice. But when you are waiting for pizza, on a bench, under a maple, in the dying light of evening, gossip becomes a script for an outdoor drama. In the middle of a story about finding an empty dinghy in the bay, a young man will stand up and say, *"Criminy! Where is that guy anyway?"* or a woman will break off halfway through a story about her loveless brother to stare down the road and mutter to herself.

Once I was waiting for pizza with an older white-haired fellow. He didn't say anything, but I could tell what was going through his mind by the way he stewed the change in his pocket. He got madder and madder until he finally banged both hands palm down on the hood of his truck, got in and tore off. Vroom. Two angry tail-lights disappeared.

Apparently, he had better things to do than wait at the bench for pizza. Not me. There's not much I'd rather be doing—especially if the kid in the Corolla is bringing me a hot feta-and-onion.

OTHER PEOPLE'S ANIMALS

August is too static for me to be entirely happy. The vegetable garden is producing heavily, but it's been doing that since mid-July. The maples and alders are at their most expansive, yet barring unseasonal drought, the foliage shows no signs of aging. The air is thick and heavy. After a brief spurt of work in the cool of morning, I abandon more productive tasks in favour of a seat in the garage, where I content myself sorting nuts and bolts into empty coffee cans.

The sole disruption in the cycle of our August days is the departure of the landlord and his family on holidays. Each year, in late August, Dave and Jean and the two children take off on their sailboat. We assume responsibility for their small farm while they are gone. Twice a day, morning and evening, Lily and I drive the half mile to feed and water the horses and cattle, muck out the barn, check the sheep and say hi to the cat and dog.

Tending someone else's animals is similar to having strangers barge into your life. Like large families of very distant British relatives who come and camp out in the back yard for the month and use electric toothbrushes in your kitchen. In both cases you quickly form impressions of which characters are unpleasant, smart, stupid, etc. Then, as the days pass and you give it more mature thought, you find that your first impressions were right on.

Take one of the horses we're currently tending. Bino is a pure-blooded mare that Jean acquired recently. I knew from previous encounters that Bino was given to snapping his teeth and flailing his head like a go-go dancer, but this behaviour I always observed from the safe side of a three-rung 2x6 fence. "Bino's frisky," I'd tell Lily, and we'd laugh.

Now I observe Bino from the same side of the fence. Each morning I have to direct her from the stall to the sand riding rink and each evening I direct her from the sand riding rink to the stall. It's an easy route that a bright rat could memorize in two minutes. But after fourteen days, Bino and I are still having problems, mostly because my right foot can't shed the memory of being stomped on by Ivy Laveck's palomino back in the summer of 1968. For her part, Bino can't stop lashing out with her hind feet, like a jackknife. Back and forth we waltz, with me pretending to be relaxed and comfortable but actually being Don Knotts, saying, "Easy, easy. Back, back," until somehow we blunder into the rink.

"Bino's funny," says Lily, as we watch the over-enthused horse snort and fart and gallop around the rink.

"Bino is a jerk," I say.

My suspicions about the dog turned out to be equally true. Huckle is an overactive, ball-chasing, drooly type of dog who tugs at his chain so hard he either chokes himself or breaks a link. (He's the one who tried to crunch our chicken.) At first I had been looking forward to taking care of him. Dave doesn't allow us to have a dog because of the behaviour of a German shepherd that belonged to a former tenant, ruining the place for dog lovers for all time. So, while Dave and family were gone, Huckle would be a surrogate pet. Any trouble, and I'd exercise it out of him.

Second day, I took Huckle off the chain. Away he went, round and round and round, vacuuming the ground, barking at dandelion balls. He was living, all right. By the time we had walked a quarter mile he was wrecked, detritus stuck on his tongue, dragging his leg like a faker. We had to turn back. So much for pets, surrogate or otherwise.

After tonight's chores, we'll have one more week of caretaking until Dave and his family arrive home. No more spastic dog, no more ornery horse. Just slow, late-summer days, deep shade, and the gentle and regular clink of nuts and bolts in the coffee can.

GOOD SOIL

I share a vegetable garden with the ghost of a dead man. The garden is seven minutes' drive from my house. Its soil is so loose you can plunge your hand in it to the wrist, so black and rich you want to eat it.

Albert died last year. I say we share the garden because it was Albert who built us the soil from the natural clays around here, year after year adding sheep manure, composted chicken manure, seaweed. Now, thanks to his efforts, my plants explode out of the ground as if in time-lapse photography.

I knew Albert for the last six months of his life. He was dying of cancer and he hired me to put up cords and cords of wood for his wife, so she'd be set for years to come. But this was spring, and even though Albert knew he wouldn't see summer's end, his devotion to the soil was such that he'd re-route me from the woodlot into the garden, where I'd till in yet more compost and manure.

It was good work, except for one thing. Albert was a former schoolteacher, and could not trust anyone to do anything without military-type orders. Trenching, hanging gates, even starting the rototiller—all had to be done according to strict procedures, which he outlined on the backs of envelopes and handed to me as if they were important documents. I still have his orders for starting the rototiller: turn gas cock on, count to five, turn gas cock off; choke on, switch ignition on, grab starter cord, and one long, even pull. The word *even* is underlined. If the engine caught, you turned the gas cock back on, and off you went. If not, the procedure had to be repeated.

Being a free thinker—especially in matters mechanical—I paid no attention and stuffed Albert's instructions in my pocket. In the case of the rototiller, the result was that I very nearly dislocated my arm attempting to get the machine started. Then I tried Albert's system. One pull, and *putt, putt, putt* ...

Between chores, I'd be summoned inside to have tea with Albert. His wife would bring it to us in the den, where he'd set up a bed, table, books. With his cup rattling against the saucer, Albert would question me about my progress in the garden. When it wasn't garden stuff it was Chekhov. He admired Chekhov, and somehow managed to change from soil to short story without a hitch. In his mind the gap wasn't so big anyway, Chekhov being to literature what a steamy warm compost is to healthy dirt.

In early March, Albert had me plant radishes and lettuce. These were the first seeds into the garden. I had to follow a map, of course, which he sketched on the back of yet another envelope. Radishes in a row, buttercrunch lettuce in a circle under glass cloches. Several weeks went by. Albert's condition worsened, so much so he wasn't able to have tea. Through gaps in the curtains I caught glimpses of him, book on his lap, staring out the window.

Albert died on a Sunday. The last day I saw him was the Friday before. I had just started work when his wife called me in. She said he wanted to see me. By this time, Albert was just a stick figure. Bedding hung over him like a coat over a chair.

"Morning Albert," I said.

He didn't have time for pleasantries. Time was precious. "Are the … are the radishes up yet," he gasped.

"You bet," I said, "they're just coming through the soil." It was true, but I would have lied if it weren't.

"Good," he said, closing his eyes. "That is good."

H*ILUX*

I bought a truck last week. A red 1974 Toyota Hilux. The right front fender is lighter than the rest of the body, being slathered in a lipstick shade of Tremclad. Colin, the guy I bought the truck from, threw in the rest of the paint, along with a spare lime-green fender, extra carburetor and well-worn repair manual, as perks to the deal. "Remember, any problems just bring it back," he hollered as I backed out his drive. "I know that truck's heartbeat."

The Toyota is the fifth truck I've owned: GMC, Chev (I called it the Blue Flame), Ford, Ford, Toyota. They were all 1) junky 2) less than seven hundred bucks (this one set me back five hundred), and—this is the important one—3) took a full day to buy.

Cars don't take a day to buy. And when I say buy I'm not talking about haggling over the price, I'm presuming that's done. I'm talking about paying the money, signing the forms, getting the keys and driving away. You should be able to do that in an hour. But it takes a day to buy a truck. People feign and fawn over old trucks before selling them the way parents feign and fawn over kids before sending them to Grade One.

Like when I bought the Toyota. Colin had owned the Toyota for eight years, and he had just bought a new pickup. That's why he was selling the Hilux, as much as he didn't want to. Being into chain saws and chicken manure and all that, I seemed like a natural candidate.

"It's all ready to go," he said when I arrived. "There's a few things I want to show you about it, though." Then he gave me a serious look, like a teacher bringing a class to order. "You might want to pay attention."

Paying attention when you're buying an old truck means going over the whole engine, part by part. Colin started with the battery and worked in. Always with the same routine: place hand on part, pat affectionately, recite a brief history—broke in 1992, rebuilt a month later, running fine since—plus necessary maintenance, then carry on.

One and a half hours later and we were under the truck, heads on cold concrete, road crud falling into our eyes. To me, the underside of a truck is like a map of Vancouver. I recognize the big parts, like the exhaust, drive shaft, transmission. Otherwise, it's a blur. But for people like Colin, it's a historical atlas of past adventures. Fingering a new tie rod, he recalls how badly worn the other one was when it broke downtown. And over there—that recently welded section of metal?—that's where he lost the muffler on the Malahat last year.

Colin took the opportunity of this last visit under the Toyota to give it a greasing, and while he was doing this he recounted some of the truck's grander moments. Like a narrow miss with the passenger train up island, or the time the truck got airborne in the Interior, and the time they climbed a near-vertical mountain near Nanaimo Lakes. How come I hadn't heard of these adventures before?

The latter trip was just last week, and as if to illustrate how rugged the truck is, Colin pointed to the part that came in contact with a very large boulder. A flange was bent double, like a folded bottle cap. "Think everything is OK?" I said, suspecting broken steering arms and out-of-alignment wheels. "Absolutely," said Colin, wincing at the injury. "You need to test a vehicle now and then."

It occurred to me that friendships need testing too, and that I might take my five hundred and depart. But thought better of it.

Finally, there comes a time to drive away. Papers have been signed, keys stripped from rings. It's a sad time for the owner, who stands in the driveway with all sorts of fond memories that probably didn't happen. It's sad for the new owner too, because this is inevitably the time you hear, "Oh, yeah, one more thing." That should be capitalized. One More Thing. Like, Oh Yeah, One More Thing: the frame is cracked. Five trucks, five times I've heard it. This time, Colin said, "Oh, yeah, I forgot to mention, reverse is funny. Treat it real gentle. Anyway, like I said, if there's any trouble, phone me. Bye."

I drove home, picking up a twenty-pound bag of cracked corn for the chickens on the way, to convince myself I needed the cargo capacity. Later that night, Colin phoned. "Just checking to see if everything went all right," he said. "Sure," I said, "everything's fine." "Oh, that's good," he said. "No, that's great."

Great? For an easy ten-mile country road run?

I think the warranty just expired.

FORTY-TWO TIMES AN HOUR

Behind our cabin, separating forest from hayfield, are three ponds. They are stepped, so water runs from one pond to another via stone spillways before exiting into a rocky stream. When I walked up there this morning, the surface of each pond was thick with swirls of fir seed, as if tie-dyed in ochre.

The three ponds are man-made, with man-made purposes in mind. They maintain the water table in the well. Water is scarce in the summer, so scarce it's the lowest common denominator of our daily lives. It determines how many loads of laundry we do per day, how many baths we take, how much and when we water the garden. It's a modest but constant test of our resourcefulness.

When we first moved here, Dave warned us that water was limited. Our notion of limited apparently differed from his, and one day, after an afternoon of uninterrupted sprinkling, our kitchen tap got the coughs. *Poof* it went and brought up something that suggested a decade of three packs a day. A sure sign, I learned, that the pump was slurping from the bottom. Dave's way of ensuring it didn't happen again was to invite me into the pumphouse to help re-prime the pump. The pumphouse has the biggest spiders I've ever seen, plus lots of sludge on the floor.

"Understand?" he said, swiping at webs in his hair.

"Yes."

This year promised to be free of water hassles. We know the well's limitations and we schedule our use accordingly. I even rigged up a garbage pail outside the bathroom window so I could siphon and store old bathwater for irrigating our expanded tomato garden.

What I was not prepared for, however, were the Canada geese. They arrived in April. Not two, as in previous years, but six. Big, chesty adults, with feet the size of fly swatters. They started off in the bay, but as soon as their goslings hatched, bald eagles appeared, snatching puffball after puffball from open water. Two weeks ago, the geese moved to our ponds.

Suddenly, the issue was water quality, not quantity. Six adult geese, I'm told by someone who claims to know, poop forty-two times an hour, or seven poops each. Add to that the droppings of the goslings, and the ponds risk becoming cesspools rather than a source of potable water.

I have been ill once before from drinking foul water. It's not an experience I'd wish on anyone. But I also like geese. They fit into the pond and its surroundings as naturally as our cabin fits into the forest. So, these last few days, I'm facing another test. Not of resourcefulness, but generosity. The geese, or us? I refuse to shoot them, as I've been told I must if our water is to remain pure, but they resist all other eviction attempts, including thrown rocks and hollering. Lorna and I even banged metal garbage can lids for an hour in an attempt to drive them out. All the geese did was hiss and bob their heads to the beat.

Yesterday I was presented with a guilt-free opportunity to get rid of the geese. Huckle escaped (again) and came snapping into the field. Snap, snap, after the goslings Huckle lunged, into the pond and out. The geese panicked and scrambled in every direction. But Dave and I, who arrived simultaneously, had the same response. We made straight for the dog and, after a few awkward lunges of our own, latched onto its thick neck. It was a reaction as simple and unconscious as making a face when you stub your toe.

"No! Huckle!" growled Dave, shaking the dog. "No."

He paused.

"Did we just make a mistake?" he asked.

"No," I said, "but we did do something dumb."

BARBERSHOP

Two months from now, maybe less, a barber is going to set up shop in Metchosin. Right across from Chuck's General Store, beside the new cafe.

This, to my mind, is the best news since Buckerfield's dropped the price on deer fence. A community without a barber is not really a community. It's a farmyard without a dog, a party without a drunk, a sandbox without a kid. A good barber sits at the head of the community table, ensuring the news and gossip are shared equally. Like a dad for everyone.

I realize these are grand claims to make of a man who smells like antifreeze and wields a pair of clippers, but I have evidence: Carl. Carl was the barber for Dad, me and all the other farmers and their kids around Dawson Creek in the late 1960s.

Carl was a World War Two vet. You could tell, because his

haircut was modelled on flat-top aircraft carriers. You'd suggest a little over the ears, and a light trim at the back. "Sure," said Carl, his clippers snip, snipping. They always snip, snipped, as if on standby. Then he mowed your head so flat it could have held books.

"Thanks, Carl."

"No problem." Snip, snip.

Carl never actually smiled, but he had four folds in the back of his big neck that grinned at you through the mirrors on his shop walls. Above those mirrors were pictures of smarmy men with out-of-date hairstyles. It was as if Carl were saying: "See all those hairstyles? Well, you can't get them here."

For my father, an Ontario farmer new to northern BC, the visits to Carl's were important lessons in local agricultural economy. Chatting with other clients in Carl's overwarm shop, he learned about planting times, harvest times, fertilizers, application rates, which co-op to sell the grain to.

All the while Carl snicked away, producing more aircraft carriers.

Carl himself never entered these farming conversations. His specialty was WWII. Infantry. Italy. Fought for every Mediterranean inch. He taught a whole generation of farmers and their sons, like me, about how to hold a machine gun, how to do crimes with a mess kit.

One story in particular I remember because it was my first lesson in revisionism, plus a few other things. It was about a time in the war when Carl and a buddy got separated from their squad while patrolling enemy territory. In the first version I heard—and don't forget this is three decades after the war—he and this fellow hid behind a rock while several enemy troops hiked past. Next time I heard the story, the other fellow had disappeared; Carl was by himself. Time after that, Carl was still by himself, but there were more enemy. Maybe five. Next time, one Carl, lots of enemy, but in this version he waited until the enemy went by then stood up and took a few shots at them. And so it went, until by the time I was well into my teens, Carl had singlehandedly taken an entire platoon prisoner, and had his sights on Berlin.

A teenager who can't get his hair cut the way he wants is not a happy customer, and one day, after hearing episode XXI of Carl's WWII, I snorted and said, "Come on."

It was a rash thing to say in the warm and congenial atmosphere of the shop. Dad snapped down a corner of *Maclean's*, and said "Hey."

Later, while Dad and I drove back to the farm in our poky haircuts, I questioned him about his remark. Carl, I said, was obviously a bullshitter.

"Maybe he is," said Dad. "But you don't talk to him that way. He's your barber."

Making Hay

The going rate for hay on southern Vancouver Island this year is $2.75 a bale; the going rate for farmhands is seven to ten dollars per hour. This is not a lot of money, but those of us who work at such jobs are paid at the end of each day, cash, by a leather-fingered farmer who strips the bills from a grimy roll in his jeans pocket. Somehow that cash (yesterday's pay, covered in dust and lint, is on the table beside me) seems more than a cheque for many times the amount. It's real, like the stick of a wet shirt on your back, or a rope burn across the fingers. To be paid any other way would be an insult to the job.

But money is only part of the reason I hay. There is also the water. At home, water is just another item on a list of pop, booze and juice I can choose from. Sometimes I go days without drinking water. But when you are haying you are basically a fleshy steam engine, and water is a necessity. Nothing else comes close.

And the water has to be good. Good water doesn't come from a tap, it comes from a plastic vinegar jug. It should be warm, so it doesn't hurt the eyes. The way to drink this water is by throwing it at your face, so some boils down the front of your shirt and some declogs the dust from your nose. Farmers know they've got a good haying crew when each person shows up with their own water jug.

One of the stranger excesses of haying is the mouse kill. Mice live in the grass and get chopped by the mower, or snatched up by predators as they dash across a suddenly naked field. This year, in a low-lying field on the Metchosin farm where I work, the swath of hay behind the mower was littered with mouse parts. Two fat ravens woofed down the remains, and what they missed was taken by a team of crows that scavenged behind.

What the mower and the birds don't get, the farm dog does. Every farm has a dog, and the dog at this farm is named Sam. Sam is a Labrador–Doberman bitch who can't stand the taste of mice (this is not uncommon) but still feels duty-bound to hunt them out. Sometimes Sam rides wing to the tractor, other times she goes sharking through the standing grass, where the mouse population grows denser and denser as the area of grass diminishes. She snaps at the mice like she snaps at bees—reluctantly—then drops their crushed bodies on the grass.

Like I said, on a haying crew, everyone works.

And then there are the courage tests. Sometimes they are as simple as who will take a tractor up the steepest slope, to the point where the wheels leave the ground and the machine teeters on the brink. Other times it has to do with the fawns that lie in the tall grass and get mangled by the mower. The farm's owner, a dump-truck-sized man named Wayne, snipped the legs off a fawn one year and had to kill it with a hammer kept in a kit on the tractor. I'd hate to have to do that; I like to think, though, that I'll have the guts to do it when the time comes.

Haying, the actual chucking of bales from field to wagon, wagon to truck, truck to conveyor, conveyor to barn, is a repetitious affair. Occasionally a bale breaks—some are heavier than others. But for the most part it's the same task over and over: lift, grunt, heave; lift, grunt, heave. And somewhere in the middle, the monster haying lunch.

Normally I'll have a sandwich and an apple for lunch. In Wayne's kitchen yesterday, I had two hot dog buns crammed with meat, tomato, lettuce and cheese; six large radishes, three raw onions, bread, a plateful of potato salad, juice, three cups of coffee, and a quarter of an apple pie with two scoops of ice cream. On the way out I helped myself to three homemade cookies. By dinner I was hungry again. Whoever said hunger makes the best sauce must have hayed.

The only time the routine of haying is fouled is when machinery breaks. If I was writing about haying seven or eight years ago, I would say broken-down machinery was part of the routine, and that it provided a much-needed opportunity to stand around, catching your breath and scratching, while the farmer burned his knuckles on hot metal.

But farms are modernizing. One farmer I worked for in Cowichan climbed into his tinted-glass, air-conditioned John Deere in the morning, turned on the FM, and that was the last we saw of him for the day. Us farmhands grunting away on the wagon knew we were haying; what he was doing I still don't know.

This year it was haying as usual—which is to say lots of stuff broke. The mower fell apart, the baler tried to bale itself, and the tractor (a mid-50s vintage International 300) started quaffing oil.

But none of this compared with Wayne's hay truck, an old OK Tire 2-ton he bought for a hundred dollars. For several hours yesterday I was taken off field duty and assigned to deliver 250 bales—125 each trip—to a farm with purebred horses and expensive cattle. The farm was about ten miles away, which meant the journey could just be made each way before the brake master cylinder had to be refilled. The truck's brakes leak (gush might be a better word), and you have to fill the cylinder every ten miles or fifteen presses on the brake pedal, whichever comes first.

"Try to drive it so you don't use the brakes," said Wayne, laying a large hand on the fender. How I was supposed to accomplish this, he didn't make clear. Like a lot of farmers, Wayne is not given to verbiage or dramatic gestures. In all the time I've worked for him, he's only raised his voice once, when he rammed a steel sliver under a thumbnail.

Everything went fine on the first trip, but on the second the brakes evaporated as I was backing down to the customer's barn. I pumped frantically at the limp pedal, and a line of cause and effect scrolled in front of my mind. The truck would crash into the conveyor, the conveyor would knock out the corner post of the barn, the barn would crash down on the purebred horses and expensive cattle, and I wouldn't get my wad of sticky bills for the day's work. In desperation, I yarded on a dinky looking emergency brake. The truck groaned to a halt. I swore, first at the truck, then at Wayne, then that I'd had my last day haying.

Two hours later, as Wayne and I heaved the last of this season's hay into his barn, the disappearing truck brakes seemed like another story to add to the list of harvest tales.

It was dark, the moon was out, and there was beer to be drunk. From somewhere in the barn behind us a mouse squeaked.

"How much do I owe you?" asked Wayne, extracting a dirty roll from his pocket.

In My Nature

There is one place on our property that causes me true grief. It's a flower bed that lies to the side of the cabin, between the lawn and a wall of wild bush. The bed is marked by a red rose at one end and a cluster of day lilies at the other. It is fifty feet long and narrow enough to reach across with a trowel.

In square feet, the flower bed is maybe .02 percent of our property. Yet it causes me a disproportionate amount of misery. More than even the water pump. Why? Because the flower bed is where nature's version of nature meets my version of nature—where chaos meets control—and I honestly can't decide which I want to triumph. Natural abundance or cultivation? Buttercups and stinging nettles, or double petunias? At times the question weighs on me so heavily that I can't even pick up a shovel.

My indecision can be traced directly to my childhood. That's convenient, I know, but it's also true. My parents shared (and still do) a love of gardening. They shared the watering can too, but otherwise, their approaches to gardening were as different as sweet peas and onions.

My dad is what you might call a cool gardener. When I lived at home, he often gardened in his underwear, and, if you looked closely amid the pots and plants, you would find a bottle of beer. His approach to nature was similarly relaxed. He once grew a complete garden, vegetables and flowers, in bush behind the lunchroom at a sawmill where he worked. Tomatoes blossomed from the middle of abandoned tires; marigolds flourished in plastic five-gallon petroleum cans. It all seemed natural to him. Even in his greenhouse at home, where space was limited, creeping ivy and the odd sprouting dandelion were treated as travellers needing shelter, rather than unwelcome vagrants.

My mother's approach to gardening was perpendicular to my father's, if not opposite. My mother is an Anglican, with strong beliefs. One of her strong beliefs is that a garden should be clearly delineated from the wilds. Each hardy annual lives in its own zone of weed-free dirt, behind a lawn she has edged with kitchen scissors. (Her hands are so strong, by the way, that she is the only one in our family who can crack a jar of Cheez Whiz without making a face.) Her flower beds are a mass of colour, but in the manner of a patchwork quilt. Reds here, pinks over there.

The source of this perfectionism, I always thought, was the religious posters on the wall at St. John's Church, where Mom and I went most Sunday mornings. They made everything look clean and trim. The Holy Land of 3 B.C. resembled Butchart Gardens of 1995. Mom clearly had an ideal and strove toward it. At night, after I was in bed, I could hear her patrolling the garden with those kitchen scissors, like Struwwelpeter, on the lookout for errant grass.

I admire my dad's approach, especially the part about drinking beer in my underwear on a sunny Sunday morning. But like my mother, I cannot tolerate the intermingling of salmonberry and gentrified David Austin old rose. It's just not in my nature.

HUNDRED-CHICKEN SOUP

Somewhere around the middle of September, the incremental change of the seasons that slowed in summer gains momentum. Flowers wilt, the maples give up the first of their deluge of leaves, and day by day the morning trip out to the woodpile is more bracing. In the never-ending cycles of rural work, it's time to prepare for fall.

This September, I'm working at a small farm up the road. I cut firewood, trim a laurel hedge and generally try to keep things tidy for the landlady, who I'm going to call Frank. For this, Frank pays a reasonable wage, plus at the end of each day she gives me two quarts of homemade apple juice. Most of this I guzzle while driving home.

I always get the juice, but I haven't seen any cash since July. Instead I've been swapping Frank goods for labour: thirty pounds of lamb and mutton for unplugging her septic line; a stack of butchering books, including Vernon Lutner's classic, *Meat Trade Secrets Exposed*, for laying plastic over her runaway comfrey patch; an antique ten-foot Kenmore freezer, one of two she hasn't used since her children moved out, for cleaning out the barn. And last week, I traded a ten-gallon pressure cooker for raking the pea gravel on her driveway.

A lot has been made of these sorts of deals—barter, my friends in Vancouver call it—and how they short-circuit the tax department and all the rest of it. But that has nothing to do with the reasons I like to trade goods for labour.

Normally, rural labourers are paid at the end of each day while standing in filthy gumboots at the edge of a hot kitchen. The man or woman of the house can't find the right change, a country music station blares, and when you pull out your wallet, a cloud of straw and lint falls on the floor. What do you do? Apologize and reach for a broom? Leave it and say nothing? I've been standing in kitchens and getting paid cash for years, and I still don't know.

Arranging a swap, on the other hand, is much more pleasant. You both go over to the item in question and, depending on its size, either put your hands on it or kick it. Then you talk, and talk, and talk. Eventually the owner gets antsy (Frank always pushes her wicker Maquinna hat off her forehead at this point) and says, "What the heck. Prune the apple trees out back and you can have it," and the deal is done.

Another thing about swapping is that you generally get better quality goods than you do buying new. When I buy something new I just go out and get it—usually from a chain store. I don't study warranties or manufacturer's specs. When you trade for an item, at least around here, you're probably dealing with a person over sixty. And people over sixty, I've noticed, are all A-students of home economics. They have favourite brands, wrap instruction manuals in plastic bags and get things serviced. The freezer I swapped with Frank, as an example, came with a well-worn green hardcover book entitled *Your*

Home Freezer and was microscopically clean. Frank says she did research before she bought it.

Swapping also gets you tips. That's something you definitely don't get when you work for cash. These tips come as accessories—a hatchet to go with the handsaw, a rack for the food dehydrator. My nephew, who also does this kind of work but is better spoken than I am and doesn't smoke, has landed some real deals: bicycles, skis, fishing rods. As a perk for yard work, a widow in Victoria once gave him a whole workshop worth of skill saws, vices and woodworking tools.

Other times, the tips aren't so tangible. Like my most recent deal with Frank, that pressure cooker. I picked it up after work one day and zoomed home for dinner. Later that night, I poked through the owner's manual (twenty-five years old and spotless) and found a single sheet of foolscap. On it was a recipe for chicken stock, written in a tight, careful hand, and addressed to me.

The recipe itself takes all of one page and half of the other side, and is a formula for large-scale soup making. It calls for three full-sized free range chickens, "approximately" forty-eight cups of water, plus a wheelbarrow full of peppercorns, onion, salt, celery (stalk and leaves) and hot chilies.

What I like is the note Frank squeezed onto the bottom of the second page. It's about how she and her husband used to buy fifty or a hundred old chickens each fall to make soup stock for winter; and how they'd starve the chickens for twenty-four hours, then push them through the mechanical plucker; and how they froze the giblets and lungs, but used the feet (scalded and skinned) to give the stock gelatin and body, and how they had soup every day for thirty years and were never sick. It's a personal essay that closes with a touch of the seasoned swapper: "If you want to try the above," Frank writes, "I can show you a quick and easy way to break a chicken's neck! Or perhaps you know?"

FALL

SPEED

*G*o to our local coffee shop these days and you'll hear about two things: the fight to ban the backyard pet crematorium up on Zodiac Heights, and the attempts by local parents to slow traffic by the co-op preschool.

I won't go into the backyard pet crematorium issue, because I'm not intimate with the details. (Although after we got a two-hundred-dollar vet bill for our five-dollar barn cat, I wished I was acquainted with the place.) Suffice it to say there is a spitting argument between the neighbours, who claim they are getting choked, literally, and the owner of the crematorium, who claims he has a right to make a buck. As he announced after the last council meeting, apparently without irony, "I wish people would just live and let live."

The preschool I know a little more about. Lily is enrolled Wednesdays and Fridays. This is her first year.

The problem at the preschool is traffic. The preschool building, an old Anglican church hall, is beside a long, straight section of road. There are many straight roads around here, but this one is especially popular for speeding because it's the first section of road that is out of Malcolm's territory. Malcolm is a longtime resident of the community. White wire-brush hair, Mediterranean features, blue windbreaker—quite distinguished. Every day Malcolm patrols a three-square-mile area of highway and road. Highways and roads in this area are his, or so he thinks. He walks where he pleases, usually in the middle of a lane, and regularly stops to stare at the sky, urinate, or both. He sounds a little odd when I describe him, but people around are so used to him they automatically slow down when traversing what's known as the Malcolm zone, then put the foot down when out of his range.

What this means, of course, is that drivers are putting their foot down right in front of the preschool. Each morning, an armada of Jettas with concrete women gripping the wheel burn past, their cars low in the butt, like an aircraft in the final throes of takeoff. Zoom. Tailgating, passing on the solid line. Then dump trucks, and army vehicles, and crabby contractors in flat decks—all hurtling by.

This parade has been going on for years. So has the annual early autumn attempt to slow traffic down. This year's go-slow program is being run by an extremely capable young father who replaced the handwritten, illegible 30 kph sandwich boards with proper signs, backed by a fluorescent cutout of a kid. He and another parent, once or twice me, shark along the side of the road, keeping an eye on traffic.

You find out a few things standing at the side of a country road and watching people roar by, which may explain why Malcolm does what he does in the middle of the lane. For me, though, the shocker was what I found out about myself. The preschool is run on the highest principles of nonviolence, co-operation, sharing and consideration. It seemed logical to demonstrate same on the road outside the school. First car speeds by, I wave my hand, palm down. "Slow down please. Thanks." Jaunty tip of the hat. Second car speeds by, wave a little brisker. Mutter: "Jerk." By the time the tenth car zooms past, the philosophies of Big Bird have been replaced with the philosophies of Jack Munro: "Hey! Get a goddamn life and slow down, asshole." After that, I found myself talking out the type of fantasy I haven't had since Ralph Pritchett punched me out for no reason in Grade Eight.

The preschool should have a gun, I thought.

No. Two guns. And a big bulldozer. That way, after you shot out the tires of speeding cars you could mash them up into Christmas tinsel!

The only thing that pulled me out of my violent reverie was my daughter, who came all the way over to the white picket fence to tell me her scab was now halfway off.

Twenty years from now, some young father will be posted outside the preschool, hollering at a gentleman doing sixty while pulling a mobile home. Maybe we could persuade Malcolm to go that extra mile, to round the corner past Chuck's store, past the body shop and the red Camaros, to the church. The kids would be safe in the Malcolm zone.

ALTERNATIVE
ECONOMICS

A couple of weeks ago my friend Mark drove out here to dig ferns. Mark is from Victoria. He wanted the ferns to put in front of the laurel he planted in front of the cedar fence he built to block off the neighbours who are always listening to one of those Oldies radio stations. So I took him up the lane, to a shady place under a maple where the sword ferns grow thick and waist-high. In ten minutes we had five healthy plants wrapped in wet burlap.

"Geez," Mark said, resting his chin on the shovel, Ken Dryden style, "you'd pay fifteen bucks apiece for those at a nursery." He paused, thinking. "You know, you should think about selling them; probably make good money."

If I had fifteen bucks for every time I'd heard there was "good money" to be made digging ferns, picking wildflowers or edible mushrooms, salvaging logs, scrapping old cars or any of the two dozen alternative ways of making money in the country, I'd be able to buy a flock of sheep—that being my latest project.

I know it runs contrary to articles in *Mother Earth News*, but there's only heartbreaking money in that kind of work.

Several years ago I was living with my friend Gordy when he decided to try picking salal. Salal is that bush florists use for filler. It was early fall, and Gordy had been laid off from his regular job as a faller. Fallers made $375 a day at that time. Gordy's UIC was better than most farm incomes. But that summer, Gordy was determined to profit from every aspect of the forest.

I was working in a sawmill at the time, so I missed out on Gordy's brief career as a salal picker. By brief, I mean two days. After which time Gordy totalled his revenue and divided it by the number of hours worked. The total: sixty-seven cents per hour. The problem, he later confided, was that he'd used his big Stihl chain saw to cut the salal, and the wholesaler wasn't keen on bouquets that smelled like gas.

But Gordy isn't the type to give up. After salal picking came grape stake fencing, hand-splitting shakes from cedar salvaged off the beach and just about every other weird way of making money you can think of. In each case, his daily return didn't pay the postage on his UIC cards.

Eventually, though, Gordy hit on a new plan for making money in the country—collecting scrap. He figured scrap was a sure thing because places like the Cowichan Valley, where we lived, were strewn with scrap middens: sawmills, gravel pits and farms. Gordy explained his business plan: "You walk around, find an old truck or loader. Then you go to the guy who owns the property, have coffee, BS for a while then offer him a hundred dollars—cash. Sell that same truck or loader to a scrap dealer and you get four, five hundred dollars!"

Gordy's first day as a scrap collector was a Saturday. I remember, because I went along. We trooped around Somenos Lake. One, two, three hours passed. Just as we were about break for lunch, we spotted a likely piece of scrap. It was at the edge of a pasture. An ancient Cle-Track 20, a predecessor to the modern Caterpillar bulldozer. Except for the six-inch firs sprouting between the blade and the engine, and the birds' nests, it looked as if it had been running that morning, until someone waved to the operator to come and have fresh biscuits and coffee.

Our impressions weren't all that wrong. The bulldozer was shut off in the morning—sometime back about 1956. And instead of biscuits and coffee, there'd been a chimney fire in the house. We got this from the landowner, a crusty old guy in a tarpaper shack we found nearby. This old fellow invited us in, made coffee, and explained that after the chimney fire it was time for haying, and then his pig came down with bursitis and, well, one thing led to another and he never had gone back to what he was doing with the bulldozer that morning some twenty years ago.

Everything was going as Gordy had planned. At just the right moment, Gordy asked casually whether the bulldozer was for sale, at scrap price. The old fellow's face dropped. "Well," he blubbered, "she's not for sale!"

Our mistake jumped on us. His idea of a coffee break was just a little longer than most people's, that's all. He thought he might actually go out and use the machine again.

"I think we ought to be heading out," said Gordy, and we beat it.

It's one thing to hoist ferns from under a maple, it's another to hoist an old man's memories, even if they are rusting in a pasture beside Somenos Lake. There isn't "good money" in either.

THE BIGGER
THE BLADE

I own seven axes. Two of them—a singled-headed nine-pounder for splitting fir and hemlock, and a lighter one with a wide blade for limbing or splitting alder—live in my truck. I also have a smaller utility axe behind the shack. Three other axes are not quite as accessible. My small, short-handled faller's axe is at the bottom of Maple Bay where I let it slip off Gourlay's wharf while cutting rope. My wedging axe is somewhere on a hill in Loughborough Inlet where my friend Billy Weddell dropped it after slicing his forehead open while hammering a wedge into a yellow cedar windfall. There may even be one at the place I used to live near Fourth and Macdonald, in Vancouver. I tucked that one into a crack in the concrete so thieves wouldn't steal it, and overlooked it when I moved out.

My favourite axe, though, sits in the woodshed. It's a fine Swedish-made double-headed falling axe: three and a half pounds with a hickory handle. It's too esoteric to be practical, but I use it often enough to have worn the manufacturer's stamp to a blur, the handle to a powdery smoothness.

My dad gave me that axe. He found the head at a garage sale and mounted the handle himself. A present when I turned thirty-two, two years ago.

It was a surprise, that axe. If there is anything Dad and I differ on, it's our regard for tools of manual labour. Dad is from a generation tied to such equipment. They used axes every day for splitting stove wood, fencing and hacking out roots. Axes were an inescapable part of life, like cod liver oil and Liberal patronage.

I, on the other hand, grew up thinking of axes as recreational: cutting firewood for beer money when I was eighteen and selling wood to finance university when I was twenty-two. Axes were fun and helped me escape the drudgery of classes. I collected several types, learned their uses and packed them around like clubs in a golf bag.

There's something honourable about a tool as simple as an axe. By extension, there's something honourable about using one. It's akin to using a bamboo fly rod. I watched with pride as my wrists thickened and my pectorals widened. I even liked it when, as a result of swinging an axe so much, I dislocated both thumbs. "Woodcutter's thumb," the doctor called it. It's embarrassing now, but I actually remember announcing to my parents that's what I was. A woodcutter.

Never mind that I was at university seven months of the year and augmented my income pushing lawn mowers. I was a woodcutter.

My dad has always had a hound's nose for frauds and posers, and he detected one in his son. One fall, just before school reconvened, he took delivery of several cords of hemlock and asked me to help split them. He had a new axe to try out, he said.

I arrived in the morning. The pieces were heaped in the driveway, "gnarly morphidites" to use the woodcutter's vernacular—big, twisty and tight-grained. Hell to split. I selected a good splitting axe from my inventory, one with a head that wouldn't get stuck, and strode in. I attacked with a welterweight's vigour. Whack, whack, whack. Around and over. I tried all the tricks: splitting with the grain, against the grain, from the middle out, around the perimeter. All we got was a shower of chips. Then Dad produced his new axe. When I first saw it I thought he was compensating for something age had taken away, or shrivelled. The new one weighed twenty pounds. It was designed not in Sweden, home of the axe, but in New York, home of the foot-long hot dog. Its simple triangular head was reminiscent of a medieval battering ram. Dad raised it up and over backwards he went, very nearly putting the axe through the hood of his new Ford Taurus (which, we now agree, wouldn't have been such a bad thing). Then he regrouped and hoisted the axe. Down it came, with great imprecision but on the wood, and the block cracked in two. "There's a lesson in physics for you," he declared, laughing triumphantly.

It wasn't until I was driving home that I realized the real lesson was more about family than physics. You don't have to have a Dad around to split the tough ones, but it sure helps.

ARTS AND CRAFTS

Country men, by virtue of the types of work they do, have a relatively easy time getting accepted into rural communities. You cut wood in the rain, clear some guy's lot with your skidder, clean your ear with a jackknife, and it's like you know the secret handshake.

Women, on the other hand, traditionally perform work that, while no less crucial to the country economy, is less public, less ostentatious. It's hard to prove yourself when you spend the summer tossing Decosonic-sealed bags into the deep freeze. It's hard to get accepted into rural communities when you don't drive tractors for fun.

I'm thinking of what Lorna has been doing since we moved here. And by connection, what my mother went through when we moved to our farm in Groundbirch.

We'd been at that farm a full year when Mom invited a half

dozen neighbour women over for lunch. The graveyard debacle had blown over, she hoped. Mom isn't blue blood, but she likes to do things right. Saucers under the teacups, cloth napkins. Maybe a centrepiece of pansies.

The lunch bombed. The neighbour women thought Mom was putting on airs. Their lunches often consisted of a can of Spam and a block of Velveeta on a plate with a knife. "Dig in, and help yourself to coffee."

My mother is slight and went to Queen Margaret's private school. And you don't fool with slight people who went to private school. One morning after the infamous lunch, Mom invited me to get out of the house and stay out. She was going to cook something for an upcoming community potluck dinner. While I fiddled in the sandbox, the smell of bacon rolled out of the house. That night we sampled the dish. It was beans with bacon. Like she never made before. These beans and bacon were so good, so perfect, that the recipe should be on that Voyager spacecraft, along with Shakespeare's plays, the DNA formula and other worldly treasures.

Mom's beans were the hit of the potluck. Scraped to the end. Even Hetti Edburg asked for the recipe. Mom held out for a week, just to make sure her status in the community was confirmed.

In many ways, Lorna's story parallels Mom's. When we first moved to the cabin we were informed that it was not possible to grow a garden. Too shady, too much clay. Only rocky old fill for dirt. I made a deal to use Albert's garden after he died.

Lorna had other ideas. She dug the clay, mixed in leaves and sand, composted diligently, planted carefully. She produced where the land had no right to produce. Enough for handouts to neighbours. That, in my opinion, should have qualified her for local status, but it didn't. Exactly what the problem was we don't know, but we suspect the garden had too many herbs. Herbs are a lefty plant.

Like my mom, Lorna is slight. She went to Magee Secondary

and you don't fool with people from Kerrisdale, I'm told. Three months ago Lorna pulled a cylindrical container from a storage cupboard. It was full of knitting needles. "You knit?" I asked. She started knitting. She did it with her morning coffee. At lunch. During preschool meetings. "Just a few rows before bed," she'd say. Sweaters, mittens, toques. Designs with swirls and checks and ropes. This wasn't recreational knitting; this was knitting with a mission. Even when the kitten came around, boot. Clickity click, clickety click.

I didn't get it. If it was money she was after, she'd be better off slinging burgers. And Lily had enough sweaters for a dozen childhoods. Then, about a week ago, the phone rang. I answered. It was a local woman who runs a craft fair. Would Lorna be interested in putting some of her sweaters in the fair? They are, said the woman, "astonishing."

I gave Lorna the message later that night, as she was knitting.

"Aren't you going to call her back?" I asked.

She smiled. Clickety click. "I'll give it a week."

CUSSING

W e had a visitor last week. Jack is from Vancouver. The second
day Jack was here, he and I were working in the garden
when I had an accident. I was screwing a hinge on the garden gate
when I slipped and drove the screwdriver into my hand—right
between the thumb and index finger. "Jesus H. Christ!" I said. I
washed the puncture off with the hose, then repaired to the house for
rehabilitation—i.e. beer by the woodstove. It was then, after things
had calmed down, that Jack offered his opinion of my language skills.
"Geez, for a moment there I thought maybe I was going to hear some
good old-fashioned cussing," he said, sounding disappointed. "But I
guess not. I've heard all *that* before."

Holy snappin' arseholes. I don't mind going along with the
country lifestyle bit—gumboots in summer and Pizza Puffs in the
deep freeze—but sometimes it gets ridiculous. Like when guys such

as Jack expect you to cuss like an Okie. What did he want? "Huh! Sacred two-headed morphidites, that hurts more than a slap on the belly with a wet fish!"

Truth is (this is what I told Jack) that cussing is a lost country art. In thirty-four years of off-and-on rural living, I've only met one person who could really cuss. That was Chris Olsen.

Chris was the oldest of three boys living on a two-thousand-acre ranch across from our farm in Groundbirch.

Chris's family and my family were friends and we'd often get together for Saturday dinners. It was on one of these occasions that we first heard Chris's acid tongue. "Do you like the new principal at your school, Chris?" my mother asked.

"Nope," replied Chris. Like his father, a black-haired man who wore belt buckles the size of hubcaps, Chris wasn't given to extra words.

"Oh dear," said my mother, and pressed on innocently. "Why not?"

"Ah," said Chris, "he's just a potlicker."

Potlicker, it turned out, was Chris's favourite word. He didn't say it often, but when he did, it came out with a great follow-through, like a well-executed slap shot. Pot*licker*. It usually caused a few utensils to drop—or at least it did on the occasion I'm remembering—and prompted an indignant "Gracious!" from his mother, Charlotte. "Gracious" was the limit of Charlotte's cussing, except for times of exceptional anger, like the time Chris cut the heads off the wrong chickens. Then she'd add the word *goodness*, as in "Goodness gracious, Christopher! Not *those* ones."

Potlicker wasn't Chris's only cuss phrase, either. There was "gol darn," and "dangnation," which were for the kind of everyday catastrophe a ten-year-old kid runs into. For more serious problems there was "Dad blame it!" which covered the scale between damnation and potlicker. (For example: "Dad blame it, Ma, I didn't know those were Grandma's leghorns.")

Chris worked at infusing his cussing with life. All three boys had large and bulbous bottom lips (usually chapped), but Chris's was the most pronounced. When he declared that someone was a potlicker, his lip went out on the *p*—slowly and mechanically, like the gate on a landing craft. The effect was one of disgust, as if Chris could hardly say the name of the person in question without spewing.

This is what I tried to explain to Jack as I sat nursing my hand. It's not my fault I can't cuss. The reason there are so few cussers around today is there are so few people who find cussing offensive. It's rare to find someone like Chris; rarer still to find a Charlotte who'll stare you down and say "Goodness gracious!"

SPLIT AND
DELIVERED OR DELIVER
AND SPLIT

For the woodcutter, there can be no better month than November. The days are cool and, on this end of Vancouver Island, relatively dry. Mornings in the woodlot are marked by the sounds of ravens, seagulls, red-tailed hawks. Always there is the gentle patter of leaves falling. If the sun is out, you might even work bare-back, as much for the thrill of cheating the season as for any need.

Yesterday, after an afternoon of just such weather, I finished cutting cords number forty-nine and fifty. Then I helped Wayne deliver them to a customer in Colwood. We'd just begun heaving the wood off when the customer—a slight guy in his forties—mentioned it didn't look too dry. "I, um, I ordered dry wood," he said.

He was right, the stuff we were throwing off was a bit mushy. What he didn't understand was that in the topsy-turvy world of fire-wood, the customer is always wrong.

Wayne paused, mid-toss. "Look, if you don't want the wood that's fine," he said. "I've got plenty of people who do." He wasn't kidding, either. One ad in the paper and we'd got enough orders to keep going a month. The customer jammed his hands in his pockets. "That's funny," he said. "That's exactly what a woodcutter said last year."

The biggest problem for woodcutters selling unseasoned cords or short cords is to get the wood off the truck and the money in the pocket before the buyer wises up. And the oldest trick to distracting buyers—men anyway—is to ask them about their woodstove.

John Steinbeck once observed that a whole generation of American men grew up knowing more about the ignition system of the Model T than they did about the clitoris. Same holds true of men today, but substitute airtight woodstove for Model T. The passion longtime wood burners feel for their airtight stoves is surpassed only by their love of bragging about them. How much their Franklin holds, how long it'll burn without restoking, all recounted with a troubadour's affection.

Wood sellers understand this, and if they see a customer eyeing a chintzy load suspiciously, they will make a casual reference about woodstoves. That is usually enough to launch the buyer on a long-winded tangent. Meanwhile, off goes the wood, into the pocket goes the cash.

There's another way woodcutters gouge customers. A real cord should be stacked very tightly, with few air spaces. Just what this means, however, is a matter of interpretation. A woodcutter in Cowichan I worked for used to tell customers that the spaces between the pieces of wood could be large enough for a squirrel to fit through but not large enough for a cat. That was for good loads. On poorly stacked loads he'd change the standard to cats and raccoons. Another trick woodcutters use is a variation on the good cop, bad cop routine that Starsky and Hutch used so successfully. Only with wood sellers it's bad dog, badder dog.

The loaded wood truck backs into a nice suburban driveway. Two toothy dogs bail out. While one heads up the street after the neighbour's corgi, the other starts excavations in the rhododendron patch.

There's your Point Grey dilemma: see three years of hard gardening ruined, or face five years' frosty relations with the lady up the street who owns the corgi. Either way, the distraction is enough to allow the wood to be heaved off and the woodcutter to collect the money.

Perhaps the best wood selling scam isn't really a scam at all— unless you consider advertisements that associate drinking beer with fun-loving chicks and muscular dudes a scam.

The idea of sales, as I understand it, is to sell an idea, a concept. Motor homes, missiles, mushy wood, who cares. It's the notion, not the commodity, that needs to be marketed. And this is why so many woodcutters drive boneyard trucks and are missing front teeth. A cord of wood from Wal-Mart? Bah. There's no chance, no adventure in that.

But a cord of wood from a guy named Randy, who returns your call from a pay phone? It's ripe.

The very best wood seller (notice I didn't say woodcutter) I've run into understood the importance of selling the image, not the product. Johnny sold wood in Victoria in the mid-1980s. His motto was: deliver and split, rather than split and delivered. Johnny drove the requisite crappy truck, with requisite dogs, and had the requisite smell. But Johnny went a step further on the image thing, and spray-painted a quote from Virgil on the side of this truck. And he kept a copy of Henry David Thoreau's *Walden* on the dash, cover up.

I sold wood with Johnny now and then, and it was as if people had been hoping all their wood burning lives to meet such a person.

"You read *Walden?*"

"On your lunchtime? In the rain? On a log? Awwww."

As if *Walden* and dirty Stanfields made for the ideal wood-cutter.

Of course those customers never wanted to discuss the finer points of *Walden,* which was a good thing, because Johnny knew as much about Thoreau as he did about ignition systems on Model Ts. But that didn't matter: the customer had bought a lousy cord from a real woodcutter. As Johnny himself once said, better that than a real cord from a lousy woodcutter.

But something makes me think customers may never catch on to woodcutters' tricks. Something makes me think that they don't want to. I've been cutting and selling firewood for sixteen years, and more than a few gyppo loads of wet wood have gone to the same customers year after year. "That wood you sold me last year was none too good," they'll say. "Couldn't burn it until February. Hope this is better." "You bet," I say. "Full cord, maybe a little more." This happens year after year. They must figure it's worth the price of a cord to see a woodcutter doing what he does best.

TOUGH KIDS

O f all the fears and worries I have about my daughter, the dumbest, yet most persistent, is that she won't be tough. That she'll simper when she gets wet cutting wood; that she'll scream when she sees a banana slug on the path to the beach. In my worst day-dreams I see our family forced from the country to an electrically heated fourth-floor city apartment where we eat lukewarm TV dinners. All because my kid wasn't tough.

Instilling toughness seems to be a Holy Grail to many rural parents, especially fathers. A kid flattens a thumb with a hammer, and Dad says, "Come on. You've got nine more fingers that are just fine. Now, hit that nail!" It's as if they're sergeants in gumboot camp.

I used to think I was brought up tough. My oldest brother Guy was the family member in charge of this aspect of my development. Guy was also, for some never-explained reason, my godfather.

He interpreted the term "godfather" in the Al Pacino sense: mean, tough. Or so it seemed to me anyway.

The summer Guy graduated from high school he leased a half section of back-in-the-bush wheat field. Several times a week he'd take me for the fifty-minute drive to inspect his crop. His favourite trick was to turn off the engine, then make a face. "Uh-oh, Tommy," he'd say, staring wildly at the gas gauge. "Look at that." Of course the gas gauge would be flat on empty. I think the idea was for me to buck up bravely to the crisis and start laying in roots for a long, cold winter. Instead, I cried and wondered aloud how I could have a brother so stupid as to always forget gas.

That summer, when I was ten, seemed to consist of a chain of Guy's get-tough rituals. During the day, if it wasn't a trip to the wheat field, he'd have me shooting cow pies. I needed a friend for this. Guy would set the two of us on either side of a fresh cow pie and have us fire our BB guns into it. We were to hit the pie at such an angle that crap flew into the other kid's mouth. (The enduring lesson of this exercise didn't become obvious to me until years later, when I went to work for one of Conrad Black's newspapers.)

Guy's efforts to toughen me up intensified as summer progressed: whitewashing the garage in August heat, haying, holding wrenches while no-see-ums drilled into my ears. No matter what I did, or how stoically, he expected more.

It all came to a flaming end just before school started again in September. One evening after supper, Guy announced that he and I were going to have a race: me on my oversized CCM, him in his black and white gym runners. The race was from the barn to the fescue field and back again, just over a half mile. We started with an unceremonious "go" from Guy—while I was still scrambling onto my bike—and he rocketed off.

I kept near him as far as the fescue field, then he put distance between us. "Ow!" I hollered, with much drama. I faltered. He slowed to a jog and I wobbled alongside. "What's wrong?" he panted. "My leg," I said. "It ... it ... hurts." I faltered again and he put his hand on the seat. As he jogged and pushed I explained in detail the disabling pain. On I went, a real first-class snivel. When he finally pushed me across the finish line by the barn, I made sure my front tire was slightly ahead of him.

"Geez," he said, bending over at the waist, "that wasn't too good, was it." His green colour suggested fresh cow pies.

I jumped nimbly from the bike and slapped him on the back.

"What's the matter Guy," I said. "Run out of gas?" It seemed like a bright quip at the time although I wouldn't appreciate a similar remark from Lily.

Parenting is nine-tenths artifice. Lily is allowed not to be tough, she's just not allowed to know it.

*I*NTO THE *B*ROTH

We've just come away from a lunch of soup and bread. The soup was a gloppy mixture of parsnips, brussels sprouts, potatoes and herbs out of our garden. Lorna and I hashed it up yesterday, then left it beside the woodstove to ferment overnight. It was so good I had three bowlfuls, and the top button of my pants has been undone ever since.

This is the third year Lorna and I have made soup. In some ways making soup together is like having a kid. You want the best qualities in both individuals to come out as a completely new entity, altogether superior to its ancestors. At least that's what we're hoping for—with our soup and our kid.

In our kitchen, Lorna handles the herbs and spices. She used to date a Lithuanian guitar player who was big on tarragon and rosemary and black pepper and the like, and Lorna picked up the talent.

In a pinch, she can scent up a cup of hot water and make it into a decent broth.

I, on the other hand, learned soup making from my mother. Her theory was and still is that a good vigorous soup can only be made by a vigorous cook. She didn't get this theory from her mother, as might be expected, but from a Czechoslovakian man who used to live next to us. This Czech made the best soup in the known universe—or at least my mother thought so. During the years we knew him, my mother noticed he always had a half-dozen concoctions bubbling away on the stove, with the result that there was a lot of cross-pollination from one dish to another. Among the things my mother says she found in the Czech's soup were eggshells, squash skins and coffee grounds. She even claims she saw him dump floor sweepings into a pot, but I think that may be one of Mom's stretchers.

My mother took the Czech's theory of soup making—if there can be such a thing—and turned it into a theory of chaos. When I was a kid, the first thing Mom did before making soup is whip up three dozen baking powder biscuits. That doesn't sound logical, until you understand that the making of baking powder biscuits is just a warm-up to the main event. It got the electrons excited, so to speak.

The main event itself took place at about five o'clock, when everyone arrived home from field or school. Trudeau was prime minister, and a heated discussion always ensued between those of us who thought he was a jerk and those who thought he was a mega-jerk. The kitchen would get hot and steamy and noisy—which Mom thought an ideal time for fusing a ham bone with split peas. Then she'd start bucking a bunch of vegetables and heaving them into a pot. During the next thirty minutes potatoes might be added, or a few dry sausages beachcombed out of the fridge—all cut up and tossed in the spirit of the old Czech. Hurried. Enthusiastic. *Vigorous.*

Occasionally I even caught Mom adding something unconventional to her brews, à la the floor sweepings. This happened when it was especially hot in the kitchen. Mom would be stirring the soup and a drop would form on the end of her nose. It got bigger and longer until—kerplop!—into the broth it went. That may sound like I'm the one doing the stretching—I know Mom's going to say so—but I saw it with my own eyes.

Now I have my own family, and a family soup recipe to go with it. With all due respect, I think Lorna's and my recipe is superior to its ancestors. Still, there's something missing from the stock: the raw vigor of my mother's soup just doesn't come through. Maybe our kitchen is too calm. Maybe we need a Pierre Trudeau to bring things to a boil. That bastard made for good soup.

A Seat at the Table of Truth

A t the centre of what is optimistically called our downtown, there is a café. And in that café is a table near the door, where a group of men, including Metchosin's oldest active pioneer, gather each morning for coffee. It's called the Table of Truth.

Early this fall, I was in the café having coffee and pretending to read the *Globe and Mail* when I overheard a conversation—and I know it's right because I wrote it down—from the Table of Truth. It was about a way of killing a goose, with a fish net, binder twine and claw hammer. The man doing the telling demonstrated with a knife and creamers.

Now there, I thought, is some really useful information. I set myself a goal: get a seat at the table.

E.B. White once said that anyone hoping to make it in New York City must be prepared to be lucky. Same holds true for

Metchosin. Not long after the café session, I discovered that my mom had gone to school with a local woman whose son needed a labourer. That son, get this, was a regular at the table. Talk about networking.

The leap from bystander to season ticket holder looked as if it was going to be remarkably easy. I'd drop into the café several mornings a week, casual-like in work gear, check in with my new boss, and order a coffee to go. The idea was that sooner or later a seat would be vacant and I'd be invited to sit down. I'd glance at my pocket watch as if making a choice and say, "What the heck." Couple disparaging remarks about municipal employees and I'd be in.

Sure enough, last week, opportunity knocked. There was an auction in Vancouver, and several regulars missed their coffee to catch the first ferry. The table was a third empty; someone suggested I sit down.

What happened after that is probably the result of me being too eager, but I prefer to blame it on a V-neck sweater I happened to be wearing. That's something E.B. White didn't say: if you want to make it in New York, leave your V-neck sweater in Boise. Or, in my case, leave it in Duncan. It's green, with trim, like Burton Cummings would wear. The only reason I had it on was that Lily was using my real work jacket as a nest for her dolls. Maybe it's her fault ...

The moment I sat down, the guy beside me, the oldest active pioneer in Metchosin, swung his back to me. Like the mechanical linkage in my column-shift '51 GMC: down and shun.

To make matters worse, the subject of conversation at the table was *The Celestine Prophecy*, and how it rated with a once similarly popular book, *Chariots of the Gods*. I do not read that type of book.

"You write," someone said. "What do you think about all this energy in the trees business?"

I shrugged. And received in return four looks of disgust, like not only did I wear a V-neck, but I was without opinions, too.

Over the next month I had a few opportunities to sit at the table, and they went somewhat better, thanks to the restorative powers of snarky remarks about municipal workers. Still, my chances were weeks apart, and that doesn't count for much. What I was looking for was a chance to sit in on the table for several days straight, to get my Union card (to use a phrase that wouldn't wash at the table).

A week ago Saturday, I had that chance. I'd sat down Thursday, I'd sat down Friday. I figured I'd go down Saturday morning and grab a spot. I managed to arrive at the café approximately seven and a half minutes after opening. Not too early, not too late.

I grabbed a newspaper from an outside box and strode in like a third-generation local. What did I see? Nothing. The table was empty save for a stack of creamers and a clean ashtray. "If you're looking for the boys," volunteered the waitress, "they go into town for breakfast every Saturday. Can I get you anything?"

Good Neighbours Don't Make Good Fences

For three days I've been working for the landlord. He has a log booming business, and the booming is done in the bay in front of our cabin. A bonus of the job is that while I bounce around with a pike pole, I can watch my daughter playing. Lily's favourite toy of late is a stick with a length of fluorescent surveyor's tape tied to one end. From out on the water all I can make out is a fluttering pink line, around and around and in and out, like a gymnast's streamer. It disappears at eleven-thirty, when I know she's conked out for lunch, then reappears mid-afternoon for another show.

"I saw you playing with your flag today," I say when I get home.

"I saw you put your leg in the water," she says.

Lorna and I have also developed a way of staying in touch while I'm out on the booms. We have laundry speak: two sheets together, good news (probably a cheque); no sheets and lots of socks, terrible news. On Wednesday I knew something fairly good had happened because two large towels were hung side by side. Sure enough, when I got home that night I found out our missing chicken had returned.

Work long enough in the country and you become multi-lingual in these nonverbal languages. Farmers have their own set of hand signals, as do loggers and mill workers. (Workers in one sawmill I worked at years ago actually developed a sophisticated set of hand signals to pass on scores from the World Series.) Speed up, slow down, go ahead, skin 'er back, smoke break, lunch break, boss is a dork—there's a whole dictionary of messages in these signals. The only part of the workday that I have never seen a signal for—and this may say something about the Canadian worker—is one that says: "let's get back to work." It doesn't exist.

But the sign language everyone around here shares is the one used when driving past a buddy on a country road. Basically, the driver's sign language can be divided into two categories. Signals that indicate irritation, and signals that indicate happiness. Actually there is only one signal for happiness. That's a little jerk of the wheel toward the oncoming vehicle, as if to say, "I'm so happy I could run right over you." This is fine, as long as both drivers aren't feeling happy. That's what happened down on William Head Road a couple years back, when two over-cheery sheep shearers steered their trucks toward each other. An acquaintance who saw the accident said both drivers were lucky to come away with their heads still attached.

Drivers' hand signals for unhappiness are more complicated. They range from four fingers slightly raised off the steering wheel, meaning "Life is the pits," all the way to a single index finger, meaning "I hope your life is the pits, too."

Observed over the course of a week, these signals can add up to a story. Last summer, for instance, I was able to measure the progress of a fence around a neighbour's yard from his little waves on Happy Valley Road. First day, Wayne swerved his blue Ford half-ton at me as if to say, "Come on over, we'll drink pop and slap up the fence." Next day I passed him on the road and he lifted four fingers off the wheel, indicating, "Hey this is a lousy job, get over here." On it went, with Wayne fencing and me not helping, until a full week had gone by. Next time, the greeting was one finger. The message was clear: "If you ever, ever want to use my welder again, get the hell over to my place and start work."

Faced with that sort of talk, I did the only thing you can do. I made like I didn't see it. And gave a little jerk of the wheel, so he'd get the message: good neighbours don't make good fences.

A Cat in the Freezer

*L*ily and I were ambling up the drive one day when we spotted a lump of feathers in the hay field. It turned out to be one of our chickens, mangled and partly eaten. "What are we going to do with it?" Lily asked. "Bury it," I said. Then, while we walked down to get a shovel, I explained how a buried chicken would turn into dirt, and dirt into worms, and worms into plants. The basic Dad Thing.

Somewhere, in the fifty acres we share with the landlord, there should be a suitable place to bury a small animal. We started digging where we found the chicken, but stopped when we realized the pond was nearby. The pond feeds our well. We tried the woods, but there were too many roots to get beyond the range of Huckle, a notorious digger. The bluff was too rocky, and the lawn had just been reseeded. After an hour we arrived back by the pond, the chicken on the shovel looking worse for its travels.

I was reminded of what happened when my Uncle Alex's cat died. Max was seventeen years old when he failed to rise off the couch in their Toronto home one morning. He had endeared himself to my uncle and aunt because he never once soiled the house. Not even when they accidentally locked him in for three days while they ice fished in Georgian Bay.

After Max died, my aunt, who is wise in an un-farmy sort of way, suggested my uncle take the body to a pet disposal place. My uncle, who is large and expressive, said it would be a cold day in hell when he paid good money to get rid of a dead cat. He said he'd bury Max himself, just like he had buried Jake, the draft horse, back on the family farm when he was a kid.

It seems to me there should be no problem stashing lifeless family members in Toronto; the CBC, for example, has been doing it for years. But Uncle Alex quickly discovered otherwise. He went out into his postage stamp-sized backyard and started digging. I guess fresh dirt in Toronto is quite a rarity, because the excavation soon attracted squads of neighbour kids equipped with Tonka loaders. Uncle Alex didn't have the heart to tell them they were digging a grave for old Max, and he left them to it.

Across from my uncle's place is an empty lot. The following night, Uncle Alex wrapped Max in a burlap sack, hoisted a shovel over his shoulder and dashed across the highway. Working quickly, he dug a hole and was almost ready to plant Max when he saw a light on in a neighbour's house. The neighbour was an older woman. She was standing on the porch, portable phone in hand.

Uncle Alex may not have had much imagination when it came to naming cats, but he could easily imagine what the neighbour was saying. "Yes officer, yes, that's right. And I haven't seen his wife for three days now..." With Max and shovel in hand, Uncle Alex dashed back home.

By this time Max was getting ripe. Uncle Alex put him in a

garbage bag and chucked him into the family freezer. During the next week Uncle Alex made several attempts to dispose of Max, including one at his office, which happened to be a fertilizer company. All failed.

Finally he gave up and made an appointment with a pet disposal service. The place had flowers, soft music and a smarmy handwringing attendant behind the counter—all things Uncle Alex hates. He put down the frozen Max with a thunk, paid the economy disposal fee of seventy-five dollars and left. As he was driving out he saw a side door of the building swing open. The smarmy attendant heaved Max, garbage bag and all, unceremoniously into a dumpster.

I know the moral of a story when I see one. And the moral here is: don't fiddle around trying to bury animals when you've got a garbage can. With Lily holding the bag wide open, I put the dead chicken in and stuffed the bag in the can.

"But why did we put the chicken in the garbage?" asked Lily.

"Because," I said, "there's no room in the freezer."

THE BLUE
FLAME

Whenever the guys get together for smart beers at Wayne's, they talk about their favourite trucks. Ford flat decks that carried double the rated tonnage, or Chevy sidesteps capable of laying rubber in all three gears. Big engines, big tires, big loads—it seems like they are recalling their favourite childhood superheroes, instead of Detroit steel.

I'm always uncomfortable in these discussions, because my favourite truck was anything but a hero. It was a dull blue 1963 Chev half-ton with an extremely worn 6-cylinder engine. That engine would propel it along at fifty-two miles per hour, and no more. The truck couldn't carry much weight, and with even a modest load, top speed was reduced to forty-eight miles per hour. It was so slow I had to pay close attention to weather forecasts, like a ship captain, to make sure the prevailing wind was always with me.

I called it the Blue Flame.

I bought the Flame from a Belgian guy in Duncan. He kept it so clean there was none of the usual archival filth one finds in used vehicles—stuff you can use to reconstruct its past. The one piece of paper I found behind the seat was a liquor store receipt. From that receipt I was able to determine that the Belgian bought Black Label beer two bottles at a time, which has to be some kind of record in Duncan.

A lot of guys claim their old trucks are cantankerous, and have a mysterious ability to break down at the most inopportune times. Like when they're fifty miles out in the bush from Clearwater, hunting deer. The Flame didn't do that. It broke down at the most opportune places. The core of the rad popped out in front of Larry's Radiators, the muffler fell off a block from Speedy, and the left rear hubcap spun off in front of Blacky's Auto Wrecking, whose motto is "Home to 10,000 hubcaps." It got so I'd fearlessly go bashing into the woods with the Flame, and cower every time we passed an automotive repair joint. A friend said the Flame and I had a classic malfunctional relationship.

I was working in a logging camp while I had the Flame. I'd drive to Campbell River and catch a flight. These trips up island were none too pleasant if it was raining. The Flame had holes in the floorboards, and filthy road water squirted through. When the front wheels were at a certain angle, the water went right up my pant leg. Same on the passenger side. To stay dry I took to wearing rain pants while driving, and carried a spare set for hitchhikers. They scoffed, until I reached the place near Parksville where the highway makes a tight S over the railroad tracks, and they got a bracing squirt. Then they'd either ask to get out, or clamber into the rain gear.

I grew fond of the Flame. On one of the trips down island from work I realized the Flame might be fond of me, too. It was night. I was near Ladysmith, almost home, when a cop pulled me over. The cop said the truck looked a little rough. He wondered aloud if it would pass a safety test and suggested I toot the horn. I thought this was going to be a problem, as the horn had never, ever worked. Neither had the emergency brake, or high beams for that matter, or a bunch of other stuff the vehicle inspection guys would love to find. I placed my hand on the horn and pressed: from under the hood came a single screech. Not pretty, but a horn nonetheless.

The cop laughed, which has to be another kind of record.

"Bet you can't do that again," he said, giggling. I said he was right, and explained how the old truck had a finite number of honks left in it, and they were not to be squandered.

I had the Blue Flame for five years. I sold it in the fantastic hope the money would seed a "new truck" fund. It didn't; the fund evaporated in a beery froth. The Blue Flame still lives, though. The woman who bought it works on a dairy farm in Duncan. A dairy maid, she calls herself. I see them now and again, driving too slowly down the highway, burdened with hay or manure, making their steady way. Always, I can't help wondering: What is she doing in my truck?

RETURN TO
THE RIVER

My family celebrates a half-dozen natural events a year—the first radish, migration of the turkey vultures, the first skin of ice on mud puddles. But most significant is the return of the salmon. Or, as we say around this house, return of the simon. (I'll explain that in a moment.)

The spawn is the one natural event we just don't miss. Which is why, even though I had to turn down a fence-building job, Lorna, Lily and I will be heading off tomorrow to prowl the banks of Goldstream, a small river twenty minutes north of here.

We've been going to Goldstream for four years now, five if we count the time we went when Lorna was pregnant. When Lily was a few months old, we wedged her into a corduroy bag on my chest and took her for a long walk under the dripping maples and cedars. I hoped she would absorb the sex-and-death pungency of the spawn, that it would embed itself in her genes.

My thinking, I confess, was partly political. Poor kid was already ingesting, sometimes literally, neon-coloured sales brochures that marked the passage of the year. Thanksgiving. Halloween. Christmas. Easter. Early recognition of the annual spawn would help counter that garish drive to consume, I figured.

A year ago, when Lily was two, I tried augmenting the trip with a lesson. I'd been reading Roderick Haig-Brown, and I was full of lore and wisdom. That's the trouble with reading nature writers; they are always so weighty and serious that you become weighty and serious.

"Salmon," I said to Lily. Articulating with lips and teeth. Dorsal fins arced through the water in front of us. "It's one of several types," I said. "Called a chum. Chum salmon."

"Simon," she said.

"No, salmon. S-a-l-m-o-n."

"Simon."

"Salmon."

The situation had the potential to degenerate into one of those things where Dad gets so weighty and serious he cuts the trip short. And spends the rest of the day working by himself in the basement. Fortunately, Lorna intervened with beer and sandwiches.

Lily's pronunciation has endured: we have simon runs, simon sandwiches, barbecued simon. Occasionally, we can afford sock-in-a-simon.

Last year I decided to take a different approach on our Goldstream trip. Instead of laying a bunch of heavy stuff about salmon names and cycles on her, I'd tell her something fun. Like the way small male chum disguise themselves as females. They do this to avoid fighting with larger males, who scrap it out for rights to swim next to a female when she lays her eggs. These, these ... what?—cross-dressers?—slide in unchallenged, and at the right time—squirt.

There's interesting nature. And if Lily took more from this lesson than I intended, well, we're a liberal family.

I never got to deliver my spiel. Before I could get started, Lily decided the most interesting part of the simon run was … the people who came to watch. Hundreds on the day we were there. Big and small, wrinkly and new, all crowding down to watch the spawn. One family even muscled a paraplegic child and her heavy chair over the rocks to water side. This, to Lily, was amazing. Two migrations: one in the water; one on the land. And that, I also confess, was something I hadn't thought of.

"Why are we all here?" she asked.

I tried to invoke Haig-Brown, failed, and shrugged.

"I don't know," I said. "It's just what we do."

WINTER

HAIG-BROWN AND
HUTCHISON

*I*t's midnight. I'm sprawled on the couch eating sardine sandwiches
and foraging through two books about country living: *A Life In
the Country* by Bruce Hutchison, and *Measure of the Year* by Roderick
Haig-Brown. Both writers are dead some years now, but I've read and
reread their works so much—and always around December—that I
think of them as friends and consider our annual get-together minor
tradition.

Last December, judging by the stains on the pages, I spent
more time with Hutchison. Hutchison is a realist. Whereas Haig-
Brown goes on about the satisfactions of growing your own food,
Hutchison admits to being scared of seed catalogues. That's right,
scared. Of seed catalogues. It's in front of me, on page 124. He
knows seed catalogues mean weeks and months of back-breaking
work. A lot of other people—me, for instance—know it too, but

don't have the guts to say so.

Hutchison is also brisk. That's another characteristic I admire. *A Life in the Country* is brimming with short sentences, brief thoughts, lousy transitions. He saws and hammers and prunes and goes ticka ticka ticka on his typewriter and falls into bed and gets up and tries to do twice as much the next day. Unquiet desperation. I like that, perhaps because this has been a mindlessly brisk year for me and I'm hard pressed to pick a season, let alone a month, of the past year that didn't disappear in a mass of picayune chores and errands.

Measure of the Year, on the other hand, is not a mindlessly brisk book. Haig-Brown's writing is even, full of cadences. His sentences are awash in semicolons. Sometimes, when I'm reading late at night, it's tempting to think of these punctuations as moments when Haig-Brown paused to strike a match, rekindle his pipe, clear his throat and pat the dog before carrying on. This all sounds great when the woodstove is ticking hot, but next morning, when you've got to face a tumbledown fence and a chain saw that won't start, it sounds like pompous twaddle.

I also like the way Hutchison does things on whim. At one point in his book he mentions climbing a tree at his Shawnigan Lake property. Bruce Hutchison was a man of some importance, writing books and editing newspapers, having scotch with prime ministers, and I'd like to know what he was doing shinnying up a tree. But he doesn't offer an explanation. He went up and down, and leaves it at that.

Haig-Brown wouldn't do that. After reading *Measure of the Year*, I wonder if Roderick Haig-Brown heaved a single bale on his acreage in Campbell River without thinking about the grasses in it, the land it came off, and the long and convoluted trip it would embark on until it was transformed into a glass of cow's milk on a kitchen table.

If it was anybody else, this would be a tiresome kind of

thinking. Somehow, though, Haig-Brown gets away with it. To open *Measure of the Year* is to get swept into a life in the country that makes sense. Hear the golden-crowned sparrow in the hedgerow? Time to plant the garden. See the half-eaten carcass of the salmon? Coons about. Guys like Hutchison and me are too busy being scared of seed catalogues for that kind of clear thinking. Not Haig-Brown. This is what he says, near the end of *Measure of the Year*, about why he lives in the country:

> I want the seasons to have full meaning for me; I want to know storm and fine weather and to have to be out in both; I want a river within sight and sound of me, the sea and the hills within reach. I want the quiet, reluctant, yet faithful intimacy of country people. I want to go on learning one tree from another, one bird from another, good soil from bad, a sound hay crop from a poor one, healthy growth from unhealthy ... I want to go on believing it is worthwhile to search for purpose and place and meaning in everything about me.

Haig-Brown wrote that passage from his panelled study in the 1940s; I'm writing from a rented shack in the 1990s. Haig-Brown went to private school; I went to public school. Haig-Brown loved fly-fishing; I hate fly-fishing. There's too much between us for me even to try to copy his style, though on wordless nights I've been tempted. What is worth emulating, though, is Haig-Brown's steadfast determination to lead his own life; to set, sight and reach his own goals, to declare himself as honestly as possible.

I couldn't ask for a better mentor, or friend.

DOGLESS IN
METCHOSIN

I need a dog. I need a dog like Colonel. Colonel was our family dog when I was a kid, back in the early 1960s. We lived beside the Cowichan River and my parents had taken an inexplicable recess from a career in farming to buy and operate a hotel. Colonel didn't approve of this career change—I think he missed the field mice—and did everything he could to express his feelings. One of his more graphic expressions of emotion took place in the fall. Colonel would wait until Mom and Dad were hosting a fancy do for all their hotel/motel tourism buddies, then he'd drag a spawned-out salmon up on the front lawn and do unspeakable things to it. The guests were agog, although even at my very young age I noticed they couldn't take anyone's word for what was going on outside. One by one they filed to the window and agogged for themselves.

Exactly how much Colonel's performance had to do with getting the folks back to farming is still a matter of vigorous debate. But the facts are hard to argue with: after three autumns of dog on salmon, Mom and Dad sold the hotel and bought two sections of land in Groundbirch, BC—as far from a salmon stream as you can get.

What got me thinking about Colonel, and dogs in general, was raking the driveway. I've got lots of better things to do around here than rake the driveway—more lounging on the couch comes to mind. But sometimes in the thick of day-to-day life I lose perspective. Little things like a few twigs on the driveway loom too large. I get obsessed with them. So there I was, in a mild December rain, frantically raking up branches and cursing the wind, and finally I saw the light. "Aah!" I said, throwing down the rake. "I need a dog!"

A dog wouldn't let you get obsessed with stupid things like raking the driveway. If you did, he'd bite at the chickens, and you'd have to go over and give him hell. When you caught him, you'd find he was actually sniffing at a rat hole under the coop. You'd get in the truck—with the dog—and drive to Canadian Tire for rat traps. Then on the way back you'd have a couple sticky buns from the sticky bun store and pick up three newspapers too. By the time you got back you'd be too full and content to care about the damn driveway anyway.

That's the thing about dogs. They keep things in proportion. They're closer to the basics of life than we are, but not so close that we can't relate. They smell good, too. There's nothing better for the winter blahs than the smell of wet dog in front of a hot woodstove.

Trouble is, I can't have a dog. The last tenant who lived here had a German shepherd that packed up with a few other neighbourhood dogs and killed five sheep down the road. This strained community relations, and Dave doesn't want to risk a rural schism for the sake of me having a dog.

All this is understandable, sort of, except that Dave has two dogs, one old, one young; the neighbours on two sides have dogs; the farmer I work for has a dog; the gas station where I get gas has a dog. Everybody but me has a dog.

Even my friend in Vancouver has a dog. Bought it a couple months ago. Up to then one of the pleasures of talking to Mark on the phone has been dropping little mid-conversation tantalizers about where we live, like, "Oh, hey, a seal just stuck its head up in the bay; no, wait, two, three seals! Wow! … Oh, sorry, sorry, Mark. What was that you were saying about the b & e next door?"

Since Mark got his dog, though, things have changed. Last time he called I was telling him about a particularly large fir I felled when he interrupted and said, "Hang on for a second, Tom. Dog wants in." The receiver went *clunk*, and I heard a door open. "Aah, you're all wet," I heard Mark say. Then there was a clicking of nails on linoleum.

Mark picked up the phone. "Sorry," he said. "Dog hasn't got any manners. Now, what was that you were saying about firewood?"

Creep. I now find myself envying a guy whose yard is the size of my onion patch, and whose neighbours need high-tech security systems. Why? Because he's got a wet stinky dog on the couch. And I don't.

Country living has the ingredients for an ideal life; all I need is a dog to help me get them in proportion.

MUD ROOMS

The busiest place in our cabin is a narrow slice of hallway near the back door. This is where we boot and deboot, heave jackets and sweaters and mittens. This is where we leave amid shouted last-minute reminders and return with newspapers and groceries and gossip too good to wait.

We call this the mud room. It's not a room at all, but its dimensions—and I mean *dimensions*—deserve the dignity of a title.

Our mud room is not a constant. It expands, like a river estuary. A high-altitude view of the inside of our house would resemble a space shot of the Fraser River disgorging into the Georgia Strait. That brown stuff? That's jackets, rubbers and runners washing into bedrooms and the kitchen.

"Lily?" I'll ask stupidly, "what are your good shoes doing by the bathtub?"

"What are your caulk boots doing by my toy box?"

Mud rooms are like cameras. They are the aperture through which events from the outside world are framed, captured. Thus when I came home with Lily in late November and said, "Lily just fell off the dock and saw bubbles," that is the way the story would be recounted for years to come.

The mud room in the farmhouse where I grew up was the best. It resembled a diver's decompression chamber: one door leading into the house and the other leading to the world. It had hard benches down either side, and smelled bad in a good, booty sort of way. When Colonel slept in there it smelled bad in a bad sort of way. This concerned Mom, who thought neighbours might come and think *Whew!*, this family smells doggy.

Mom, we said, they all have mud rooms.

In fact, as I sit in my kitchen now (looking, incidentally, at a pair of muddy gumboots), I'm pressed to think of a significant event that didn't happen in that mud room. It's where the police officer told my father his mother had died; it's where we first met the woman who was to become my brother's wife. The mud room is where I first learned that Moms could, well, put their own spin on things.

I had just come in from playing for hours in the snow. My boots were jammed. I tugged at each, then Mom tried. She used both hands, then sat on the dirty mud room floor with her feet against the bench and yarded until she was red. I began to cry, softly, then harder. "Cold?" she said. "Yes," I sobbed, "and I don't want anyone to know, either."

She pulled again and made a face. "Don't worry," she said, "we'll tell them our own little story."

One thing mud rooms do not do, however, is lie.

My brother Paul discovered this when he came home late for his seventeenth birthday party. "Sorry," he said. "Car broke down."

He was in the mud room of our farmhouse. We—Mom, Dad, brothers, Colonel—had gathered in the mud room to hear why he was coming in at nine for a six o'clock dinner. But something about this story didn't ring true, and Dad inquired further. Turned out the car had broken down because Paul had run it into a telephone pole outside Pouce Coupe.

From then on, the tale of the Paul's accident was always recounted with another tale, about how he tried to BS the family in the mud room.

NOT BEING
WET

I have hung up my rain gear. At the back of the garage, beside the old CCM 10-speed I never use.

It's not that I'm done cutting wood; unless there's an unseasonable warm spell there will be orders until the end of February. And God knows the rain won't stop. But I'm done with the rain gear—for this year anyway.

To wear rain gear you have to be an optimist. I lost what vestiges of optimism I had about rain gear last week. It was a wet morning, and I was getting ready to fall trees on the woodlot where I work. I was cinched into my rain gear, my head was dry under the hard hat and I'd had my morning tea and sandwich. Fine. Even my toes were warm. Then I looked up at a tree. A little stream—let's call it a freshet—poured out the back of my hard hat, into my collar, and tumbled down my back and into my pants. If I hadn't been strapped for rent, I would have quit on the spot.

Every year I try wearing rain gear; every year I have to be reminded what lousy stuff it is. Rain gear doesn't keep you dry, unless you're standing around doing nothing—i.e. being a foreman. You sweat so much inside you get soaked. But instead of smelling like Pacific coast rain and wood chips, you waft sour fumes, like you've been on a month-long diet of pickled herring and Danish Aquavit.

Rain gear also has a way of making you useless for work. You know how guys are when they get a new 4x4? Won't take it to the mall, let alone up the mountain. The same is true of new rain gear. It is an observable fact, for example, that a logger in new rain gear does half the work of a logger in old rain gear or no rain gear. A logger in new rain gear is afraid of chain saws, poky branches, wire rope with jaggers. He stands erect and goofy. Useless. This goes on for a day or two, then he slips or slides, gets the rain gear dirty and ripped, and carries on with work.

There is the occasional exception. One guy I worked with in Phillips Arm managed to keep his rain gear intact for a month. That's a record, if there is such a thing as a record about rain gear. We nick-named him Cottage Cheese, because he was a younger and smaller version of his brother—a foreman we called, for forgotten but probably obscene reasons, Cheese. Cottage Cheese was so fastidious he combed his hair at lunch. First day it rained he pulled out new rain gear. It fit perfectly, of course. The rest of us looked like garbage bags with wet hair on top; he looked like a Zeller's model. It rained for a month straight, and for a month straight Cottage Cheese moved as if he had chronic back pain. Slowly. Carefully. At first we tried to get him to do things that would rip his precious rain gear, then after a couple weeks, we began to cheer him on in his struggle, like you cheer the untouched car at a demolition derby. Finally, around week four, Cottage Cheese lost his fight. He slipped on a log and a knot sliced his pant leg from hip to cuff. It didn't seem like a big deal to us, but he considered it an insufferable indignity. He finished out the shift, and that's the last we saw of him. Couldn't have been strapped for rent, I guess.

Now I wear wool, right next to the skin. That's the way to stay warm when you're wet. It was Gordy who first explained to me the alternative to rain gear. Gordy said wearing wool next to the skin was the best way to stay warm. He even had a theory. The problem with working in the rain, he said, was not being wet but getting wet. It's all the same, once you're soaked through.

"And what about living in wet clothes?" I asked. "Isn't that a prescription for arthritis?"

"Nothing WD-40 can't cure," he said. So heartily did Gordy believe in his theory that he didn't even dry his clothes at night. He climbed into the wet, clammy stuff every morning.

I'm not that tough. Since giving up on the rain gear I make a habit of hanging my work clothes around the woodstove as soon as I get home. Then I shake out my hair and listen to the drops hiss on the stove top. Soon the cabin smells of wood and sweat, but I don't mind. The best part of coming home after a day in the rain isn't being dry, it's getting dry.

A Single
Scintillating Call

One evening soon after we moved here, Lorna and I were in the living room reading. It was January, and a southeaster was blowing so hard the drainpipes outside moaned like breath across an empty beer bottle. The woodstove was ticking hot, the cat was dieselling on the couch—everything was snug and safe, just as we dreamt it would be when we left the city.

Lorna lowered her book—something linking postmodernism with perennial borders. "You know what I could go really go for?" she said.

I lowered my magazine. "No."

"A couple good reruns of *Dallas*," she confessed. "Then I'd like to watch some Letterman. Remember him? And some news; I'd like news with war footage from helicopters and all that."

At first I was disgusted. Part of the reason we moved here is you can't get TV, and the nearest newspaper is fifteen minutes away. But then ... then I realized I could go for some *Dallas* too. Plus some Letterman. And I wanted reruns of something. "How about *Hogan's Heroes*," I said, getting into Lorna's slipstream. "Yeah." she said. "And *Street Legal*." This started a long conversation in which we wallowed in the theoretical satisfactions of vegging out with TV and cheap ice cream and the stuff we hadn't done for ages. Doing without good mindless entertainment is one drawback of living beyond the reach of big media.

Just the other day my brother introduced me to another. Hugh was describing his feelings about carpentry by comparing himself to a sitcom character named Jason.

"Jason? " I said. "Who's that?"

Hugh looked at me like I was Geoffrye Chaucer. "Never mind," he said.

This is not to say there aren't any advantages to doing without TV. It's just that the advantages are not the ones that come to mind, i.e. peace and quiet staring out the window. I gave that up months ago, because every time I looked out the window I saw something needed doing, and felt guilty.

When you don't have TV you get the joy of seeing the world through other people's eyes. Sports, for example. Whenever something big happens in sports, my mother-in-law Edith phones. Last time this happened was when the Canadian hockey team won the world championship. In the course of three hours we got four phone calls, each updating us on the score. On the last call Edith described how one of our wingers had deked the opposition goalie and, as she put it, "threaded the needle and hammered it home." This may sound dull compared with TV, but actually it's the opposite. TV, as anyone who has watched a real hockey game knows, speeds up the play. Edith goes one step further, encapsulating the game in a single scintillating call.

This year, in an effort to find a middle ground in the TV–no-TV debate, we bought a VCR. The idea was we would buy buckets of blank tapes and distribute them to our friends who do get reception, on the understanding that if they saw something we'd like, and taped it, we'd pay them back with a dozen scratch eggs. What we found, however, is they all think we are serious types. They send us *Masterpiece Theatre*. Either that or programs on how to enhance the performance of your composter.

For three months it looked as if our craving for junk TV was going to go unsatiated. Then, accidentally, at the end of a million hours of *Middlemarch*, a friend included an episode of *Star Trek: The Next Generation*. We watched it once, and have never been tempted again. We're happy enough knowing it's there.

TOBACCO

*I*went on my semi-annual walkaround of the place the other day. Walkaround is what I call those rare mornings when, instead of stepping straight out the back door and onto Lily's Little Tyke tractor, I stop and ponder the toy instead, and say to myself: "Geez, I was going to build a sandbox for things like that six months ago. There's something else I didn't get done." A walkaround is a quiet, somber process, conducted with a mug of coffee and a cigarette before the rest of the family is up.

As usual, the results of my latest walkaround weren't impressive. Oh, I noticed the odd success. Like the chickens. Before we got our modest flock, people told us chickens were a dumb idea and that we'd spend more on feed than we'd get for the eggs, and the birds'd just get eaten by hawks anyway. Well, not only do we have all but one chicken, but we've got thirty-two dollars from egg sales in a

Miracle Whip jar on top of the fridge. Also, we have fresh eggs (they're still warm when we put them in the pan) as many times per week as we figure our arteries can stand.

Of course, we don't have pickled beets to go with the eggs for breakfast any more. Pickled beets are one of the failures this year. I like pickled beets, especially with eggs and potato sausage. I found a killer recipe in April and put up enough pickled beets to last all year—or so I thought. I ate the last jar watching the Grey Cup.

After the eggs, the plus side of the ledger gets pretty thin. Sure, I had the sense to cut enough firewood to cover the side of the garage last spring, but against that is a long list of incomplete projects: the trim on only one side of the cabin, the unfinished rock wall, the rats I didn't trap, the latch on the deer fence gate I never attached, the raccoons I didn't evict from under the deck, the rodent-proof compost I didn't build, the cat we didn't get spayed, the tobacco crop I wrecked.

That tobacco will always bug me. Last February, a friend in Vancouver sent me a few tobacco seeds in a film canister, because he thought I might want to grow my own from his family's private stock. I got to figuring. Four smokes a day comes to about twenty-five dollars per month on tobacco. That's three hundred dollars a year. I thought about how happy I'd be with a homemade cigarette in my mouth and three hundred-dollar bills in my pocket. It was too good to resist. I planted the seeds with care.

After broccoli and spinach, it was fun to grow something that wasn't good for me. I studied literature on tobacco, ordered government pamphlets and talked to everyone who knew anything about tobacco. This led me to my dad, who was raised on a farm around Chatham, Ontario, which is prime tobacco country. Dad got so interested in what I was doing that he took several plants for his greenhouse.

June turned to July, July turned to August, and our tobacco

plants were ready for harvest. They were giants, each eight feet tall and thick with big, yellow leaves sticky with nicotine. I used an axe to chop down my plants. Dad harvested his leaves too, and presented them to me in a bundle tied with string. It was a busy time of year, so I hung them in the garage and forgot all about them. Until, that is, my walkaround. That's when I decided to see what sort of tobacco I'd grown.

To describe that first puff, I'll ask you to return to that day in your youth, probably when you were ten, when you and a friend snuck out to the wooded area behind your house, rolled up some maple leaves, and smoked them. Remember that searing feeling in the back of your throat—like you'd been shot in the tonsils with a pellet gun? That's exactly how it felt when I tried my homegrown tobacco. Rotten, vile stuff. I still gag thinking about it, and about how much work went into growing the plants.

There is one consoling thought about the tobacco disaster. Where would I be today if the tobacco had been as successful as my pickled beets?

JOBSITE
EVANGELISTS

A hazard of working as a casual labourer is that you're a mark for jobsite hustlers and evangelists. It's as if getting hit on is part of the work, like providing your own work gloves, or lunch.

Take what happened at a fencing job I was on last fall. It was my second day. Three of us, two regular hands on the farm and me, were perched on the pickup tailgate, having coffee. We were talking about how expensive it was to run a vehicle. One of the regulars, Fraser, casually leaned ahead, cleared his throat and said, "Do you really want to make some money, Tom?" He was pointing a finger at me and doing his best to look earnest, in a financial sort of way.

That's a sure way to tell you're being hit on, when they try to look financial. Another way is when they make illogical transitions, like: "I see you're having trouble hacking through that hemlock root; thought about putting your money to work for you, instead?"

Fraser went on to explain how, for a mere hundred dollars, I could get myself in on a unique money-making proposition. All I had to do was get two other people to cough up a hundred bucks each. From then on I'd be a middle manager, and gradually move to the ranks of the filthy rich.

Call me a hypocrite, but I don't take financial advice from mud-stained farmhands. Furthermore, I know all about those pyramid investment deals, having been bilked by my math teacher when I was in Grade Nine. I said as much to Fraser, and made it clear that if I heard any more money-making schemes I'd leave him and his partner to hack the fence through themselves. That's one advantage of labouring jobs, you can toss them off like baling twine.

Dismissing a co-worker who hits you up for religion is a little trickier. I'm thinking of a time when I was hired on at a log yard in Chemainus. The yard had too much wood, and I was to help a red-haired old shake bolt cutter named Harry chop up a pile of cedar. Harry and I had worked side by side for several days when, just before lunch, he rested his axe on a block and said, "By the way, did you hear about the scientists in Phoenix?"

It sounded like the lead line for a dirty limerick. I said no, I had not heard.

"Well," he said, "they discovered beyond doubt that God exists. Proved it, right there." He made it sound like a cure for hiccups. He went on to explain how those Phoenix scientists had also proved that a finite number of people were going to be saved at the end of the world. Harry, it turned out, was a member of that religion whose members often knock at your front door, usually when you're watching football. He wanted me to join the church. I said no. So he kept on talking.

During the next week he talked so much that he went past what I think is the gobbledygook of religion and got to the good stuff. He used to be a drunk, he said. Twelve beer and three fist fights a night in Prince George. The church helped him dry out. He used to be lonely. Cry in his truck. Now he had friends. The only problem, he confessed, was that the church required that he hit on so many non-believers a month. That was difficult for him to stomach.

I have many friends, some I've had since grade three. None has been brave enough or humble enough to tell me he's cried in his truck. I liked Harry. So I made a suggestion. A proposition, even. I said he could hit on me as many times as necessary to make his quota, as long as he stayed away from my place when football games were on. "Who knows," I said, for fun, "maybe I'll even join your church."

"Maybe," said Harry. The two of us dressed in matching suits and haircuts, going door to door, big smiles the whole time. Enough to make a guy cry in his truck. "Maybe not," said Harry.

I realized later it was a good thing Harry didn't take me up. Like all the other jobsite hustlers and evangelists, he needed the challenge.

ESTATE CARS
REVISITED

Three months ago, when Lorna's dad passed away, we inherited his car. A 1979 Chevette, four doors, low miles, brown like chocolate milk.

At that time we were too broke to afford insurance so I parked the Chevette between the compost and the woodshed. When people asked about our "second car" I corrected them, and said it was our "spare" car. Anyone can have a second car. But a spare car? That sounded like something good, self-reliant country people would have, along with a root cellar full of turnips and extra shells for the 30-30. I had visions of my father's Ford Taurus detonating in our driveway during a visit, and me consoling him as the pieces rained down like autumn leaves. "That's OK Dad, that's OK; I've got a *spare* car you can use."

In its first months of off-the-road life, The Brown Car—as

the Chevette soon came to be called—simply sat in our yard. If it did have a use, it was only to steady ourselves as we watched a pair of mallards whistling overhead. Then, slowly, it came to be a repository for various items: chicken feed, a bale of hay, wild bird seed, garden stuff, paint thinner. One day I even left a crab in there.

The Brown Car began to smell. But the smell wasn't a stink, as might be expected. Instead, it wafted a pungency that appealed to a primitive instinct—the same instinct that makes men sniff their dirty socks. I took to having my morning coffee in the car, door open, one foot on the ground, breathing deeply, listening to the birds.

About this time I began driving it—although still on the property. First, to check the mail; then to take Lily and zoom a dozen eggs to the landlord; finally, just to roar spontaneously around the property, pushing over little alders, having fun.

After these quick excursions I'd extract the keys, reef on the emergency brake, and let Lily sit in the driver's seat to play, where she'd reenact our circuit.

One day about a month ago, Lily emerged from one of these sessions in the Brown Car holding something. It was the signal arm. Turns out she'd been playing Ms. Logging Truck Driver, and yarded the stick right out of the steering column. Normally this would be cause for weighty discussions around here. That's what Lily looked like she expected. But my response surprised both of us. "Hey," I said, "that's neat, I didn't know there were so many wires in one of those things." It was at that point I realized something had happened to the Brown Car, that it had entered a state where we no longer cared about details like turn signals. It had become ... an estate car.

Now I know the joy of running an estate car myself. The joy of hurtling around in a car with no plates on the front and twenty kilos of chicken scratch in the back is the joy of a three-year-old fresh out of the tub, running bare bum around the house, squealing. An estate car is a regular vehicle with its clothes off.

Alas, the Brown Car must go. We need the money, irony of ironies, to keep our main vehicle, a nondescript asexual Mazda, on the road. I figure if I ask four hundred bucks it ought to move quick enough. The only trouble I'm having is coming up with a pitch that does justice. What am I supposed to say: "For sale, 1979 Chevette, four-door, low miles, smells good—like an old sock"?

PROJECTS

*L*ily is entering the project stage. She wants a swing, a playhouse, a slide.

I'm of two minds about kids' projects. The sensible side says go to the building supply store, buy a two hundred and fifty-dollar yellow plastic tree house, and be done with it. The other side says take Lily to the beach, scrounge lumber, help her slap up some walls. For a roof we could take the hood off that '62 Sunbeam that died in the cow pasture a few years ago, and spike it on. If she flattens her thumb in the process, well, to my way of thinking that's just a perk to the deal.

I've been an advocate of the bang-your-thumb theory of education since I hung around with the Olsen boys. Olie and Charlotte Olsen didn't exactly encourage the boys to get in trouble, but they didn't discourage it either. I'm thinking of the time the Olsen boys decided to dig a hole. Not for any reason really, except that all those Steve McQueen World War Two escape movies were on at the time, and the idea of tunnelling seemed kind of cool.

So they dug. They started on a Saturday morning and by the time I joined them for a Saturday night sleepover, only their pig-shaved heads showed above the ground. First thing next day, four of us started in again. By this time Olie had given us a pick and some shovels. (I remember thinking his belt buckle would make an ideal scoop.) Charlotte Olsen helped too, bringing snacks of cold pancakes and peanut butter, pitchers of chilled Freshie. Come late afternoon we were down eight or nine feet and every time one of the parents or a farmhand came to peer down at us, their feet caused a little avalanche to fall on our heads. How deep we could have gone is any-one's guess. But the oldest brother, Chris, had the idea of sinking a horizontal shaft—a drift, I think miners call it. Our intention was to get to the farmhands' bunkhouse and scoff their *Playboy* magazines. The drift collapsed and the youngest brother, Roger, got a face full of dirt. Even then, the only thing Mr. Olsen was mad about was that it wasn't one of us older boys who was in the tunnel.

While a farmhand filled in the excavation with the front-end loader, we shovelled manure—shovelling manure being the standard form of rural discipline.

The Olsen boys could pretty well do what they wanted in their bedroom, too. They shared one room, an addition to the house made expressly for that purpose. It was set up like a bunkhouse. Bunk beds here and here, and a fold-up cot there; lots of beds for anyone who wanted to sleep over. The walls were unfinished, unpainted planks, secured to studs with four-inch spikes. The floor was made of the same material, which ruled out socks or bare feet, unless you wanted to deal with an eight-inch sliver.

The parents' attitude toward this room was: anything goes. Only power tools and matches were prohibited. Want to pound a spike into the wall? Go ahead. Wish to carve your name in the floor? Fine.

This rough-and-tumble approach to parenting taught the kids to be resourceful—an invaluable skill for country living. One winter night when I was visiting, the boys decided to cut a hole in the floor. I can't recall exactly why we wanted to do this, but it probably had something to do with Steve McQueen and the *Playboys*. So we gouged and drilled until a keyhole saw could be inserted, then cut a hole big enough for our scrawny shoulders. Down we went, and goofed around under the house until nine o'clock, when it was time to go to bed. Then we discovered something. The bedroom was cold. Cold air isn't supposed to come up, but it did. How to stop the flow? Chris had the bright idea of convincing Roger it would be neat to sleep on the floor. That's what real soldiers do, explained Chris. We all slept until Roger woke up screaming from the cold. That was good for a half day of shovelling cow manure.

This brings me back to Lily and her projects. My thinking is this: if she has fun in a playhouse we put together, good. If she slaps on an addition herself, that's even better. And if her hammer comes down—accidentally—on the cat's tail … well, the chicken coop always needs cleaning.

MANIFOLD
DELIGHTS

Whater you work outside and eat your lunch outside, as I do, you have a choice. You can accept that you are going to be eating in the rain, probably perched on a stump, and pack a simple, sustaining meal. Or you can pretend you won't be in the rain, on a stump, and pack all sorts of fancy sandwiches and pickles and cookies.

I favour the former. My lunches consist of a large block of cheese and a half loaf of bread wrapped in wax paper. Occasionally, I'll add a large raw onion. Taken with a thermos of cold water, cheese, bread and onion is a fine lunch. The tastes match my thoughts when I'm working hard: plain, direct, uncomplicated.

Gordy doesn't see things this way. Gordy is at the opposite end of the spectrum when it comes to lunches. He's of the opinion that lunches are supposed to be uplifting experiences, culinary adventures

126

that take a working man's mind *off* the job, not further into it.

The first time I worked with Gordy was in a dryland sort in Chemainus. I was cutting shake bolts, and Gordy and his dad got hired on. This was a piecework deal; work as much or as little as you liked, you only got paid for what you did. Halfway through their first day, Gordy and his dad broke for lunch. Most of the other shake cutters either went to the Horseshoe Pub in Chemainus for a meat loaf sandwich and draft beers, or they did as I did—took quick bites from an abbreviated lunch and kept on working. Then, as now, I preferred cheese and bread.

Neither of these options was good enough for Gordy or his father. They opened the back of their Toyota Land Cruiser and unpacked a modest-sized deli. Brie, Swiss and Stilton cheeses, watermelon juice in coolers, sliced meats, those little wieners in a can—all spread out neatly on an oilcloth. Van Morrison crooned out of the speakers. They even brought their Airedale, who perched nearby waiting for morsels. The rest of us couldn't believe our eyes. What was this, the company picnic? We glanced at each other and smirked, thinking these two were better suited for another career—like hairdressing.

We were wrong. Over the next few months, Gordy and his dad averaged six cords a day, which was as good as the rest of us. The only difference between us and them was, they abhorred sandwiches. They said a working guy's lunch was too good an opportunity to waste eating Spam between two slices of boredom. "Once I start thinking about what I'm going to have for lunch, the day's as good as over," explained Gordy.

The next time I worked with Gordy was in Phillips Arm. By this time he'd advanced from buffet-style lunches to hot stews. He would dump everything from the cookhouse lunch counter into tinfoil and fold the foil tightly. Later, up in the bush, he placed the foil bag on or near the manifold of a piece of logging equipment and let it cook. Not only were these "manifold delights," as he called them, good, but they were never the same. Each day's lunch was a steaming potpourri of meats and vegetables cooked in their own juices. That's what Gordy said, anyway.

So seduced was I by the idea of a hot, stewy-type lunch that I skipped my usual bread and cheese and tried one of the concoctions myself. My manifold delight was a dog's breakfast of sauerkraut on tuna on mozzarella on lasagna on pancakes. All boiled into an oleaginous glop. Two spoonfuls and I decided to call it fast day and chuck the rest to the ravens.

Which brings me to the last time I saw Gordy—ten days ago. We were bucking logs in a mill about fifteen miles from here. Gone were the fancy wieners, gone were the manifold delights. Gordy had simplified his palate. Every morning he stuffed his pockets with jujubes and wine gums. During the day he always had something to munch on.

Not being a big jujube fan, I found it easy to resist this idea. Still, work day in and day out beside a guy, and even his worst habits become fascinating. One day I asked Gordy if he had any extra candies. He said sure, lots, and produced a handful from a chip- and lint-filled pocket. I stuffed the candies in my mouth, forgetting that when you're using a power saw all day, your pants get soaked with gas and oil. A couple chews and ... *Eecht! Ptooey!* I struggled to get the stuff out of my mouth, licking at my chops like a dog that's just eaten a mothball. This went on for several minutes. Finally I was able to look Gordy in the face. "You don't like those things, do you?" I said, still spitting.

He grinned and popped another one into his mouth. "No," he said. "But they sure keep your mind off work."

Gordy and I agree that food is an important part of work. Where we differ is in purpose. He wants it to keep his mind off the job, and I want it to keep my mind on the job.

BAD GUYS

The worst guy in this community, the baddest, meanest, dirtiest no-good, is a 6'2" carrot-haired fellow called Bert. The name Bert doesn't really do his character justice; if this were the 1920s he'd be called Black Bert, or Cattail Bert, for what he did to the neighbour's tabby.

Bert will be moving in a week. He's taking his family, heading to Port Hardy. Some people are saying, "Good riddance, we don't need Bert's type around here." But not me.

It seems to me bad guys like Bert are a necessary part of any community. They're a reference point for behaviour, just like the community do-gooder is on the other end. Most of us aim for somewhere in between. I've known a few guys like Bert. The Leblanc brothers, for instance.

The Leblancs lived down the road from our farm. You could

tell they were bad news just looking at their yard. Tarpaper shack, landscaped with garbage and humping dogs. Beside the shack was a tripod of fir poles, for lifting engines out of old cars. A tripod of fir poles in that country meant the same thing as the Confederate flag in Alabama. Spread around this tripod were the carcasses of cars and trucks, many of which were upside down.

The Leblanc brothers were no treat to look at, either. Lyle, the younger, had taken a boot to the face and broken his nose. He'd never had the nose set, so the bone jutted out like armour plating on a brontosaurus. Brother Wade was scarred, too, but he had the rough appeal of a torn pair of blue jeans. Artful rip on the cheek, missing tooth. Young women found him attractive, much to the distress of their parents.

The Leblancs could be found in one of two places. In uninsured cars with no hoods, hurtling along dusty country roads; or back of the log hall at community dances.

For most people, these dances were a time to forget fallen fences and have fun. Adults danced until midnight, feasted on potluck stews, then danced again. Us kids ran until we passed out on heaps of jackets under the tables. The Leblancs, on the other hand, seemed intent on making everyone have a lousy time. They stood at the rear of the hall, backs against the rough logs, sneering. Their spell became so pervasive that all the other young guys took to leaning against the wall and sneering, too. Over a couple years the end of the old hall actually sunk eight inches. The only time the Leblancs left the wall was to go outside and chug-a-lug rye and have a quick fist fight.

It seemed the Leblancs' goal was to kill the dances, and one January night they almost succeeded. Halfway through the evening, Wade Leblanc staggered onto the dance floor. This was unusual, but everyone figured maybe he'd lightened up. He was kicking up his feet and stomping, which was the basic country dance, when his cowboy boot shot off. Then the smell hit us. Feces. Stuck on his wool sock.

That's vile, I know. But guys like the Leblancs do vile things.

Turns out brother Lyle had crapped in Wade's cowboy boot and Wade, to prove how tough he was, had ignored the squish and carried on.

The dance paused; a couple kids gagged. Wade flashed a smile to his brother, like, "This will get 'em, Lyle!" It seemed like it might, too. But what the Leblanc boys hadn't counted on was all the people who aren't mean, or bad, or dirty no-goods. They hustled those rotten Leblancs outside; others gave the floor a wipe and the dance carried on until dawn.

Next dance, the Leblancs were barred at the door, which left them in a dusty parking lot full of untended vehicles, which wasn't so smart. The brothers didn't miss much inside the hall, either. The festivities sputtered and died before midnight. There's the point. It doesn't make sense to celebrate when rabble rousers like Bert finally leave town. Because you can't have a dance, just the way you can't have a community, without bad guys.

A NET NAMED GUY

M y oldest brother just sold his sawmill. Guy's mill was a rusty sheet metal and iron affair just off the highway in Chemainus. It was often broken down, but it had been in the family so many years it had become a fixture. "Guess what? Guy's sold the mill," is how one of my other brothers broke the news to me. He might as well have announced that the federal government was cancelling the whole unemployment insurance program—as of yesterday.

Guy and Guy's mill were the family safety net. The rest of us work in seasonal occupations—logging, farming or combinations thereof—and inevitably are unemployed several months of the year. That's the worst part of these jobs. With Guy's mill, though, you didn't have to worry about unwanted lay-offs. You'd just phone him and ask if there was any work. He'd hem and haw on the phone and eventually say yes. If he didn't say yes, Mom would get on his case and not invite him to family dinners. Family dinners are the only time Mom makes pork and beans, and pork and beans are to Guy what No. 1 alfalfa is to a dairy cow. So he always found us a job, even if it was shovelling chips.

There are advantages to working for family. For one, you get to make huge mistakes and don't get fired for them. The mistake I'm thinking about was swinging a flat-bottomed chip shovel at Guy's head and yelling that he wasn't paying me enough. I was fresh out of school and had taken exception to the fact that men doing the same job as I was were getting two bucks an hour more. And the only thing they did better was take long coffee breaks. Guy said I was too young to be making adult money, and in the heat of the ensuing argument I swung the shovel at his head. Try a stunt like that on a regular boss and you'd be down the road.

Another advantage of working for family is that you can be brutally honest with the boss. On regular jobs you only get to be honest with the boss once a year—at the annual picnic, when the apple cider is flowing freely. In a family operation you get to do it every time there's a family get-together, which for us was every two weeks. Whoever happened to be working for Guy would back him against the Frigidaire and tell him what he was doing wrong with the head rig and how he could get better life out of the chipper knives and blah, blah, blah. All he could do was keep on scraping his spoon on his empty bean bowl and watch for a chance to get a refill.

From Guy's point of view, having a big family to draw on for labour wasn't such a bad deal either. We were decent workers and were willing to go a couple weeks without paycheques if the need arose. During really tight times, like the recession of the early 1980s, we worked a lot of overtime for no charge. I did a stint at the mill around that time and was up before dawn, fumbling with my work shirt in the dark, so we could have the mill ready by the time the regular crew arrived. It seemed heroic in a family sort of way.

All this isn't to say there weren't drawbacks to working for family. For one thing, the regular workers always thought we were in on nepotism. This was true, I suppose, except they were never there early enough to see us doing charity work for the company. The other drawback is your boss can be brutally honest with you. Which is something else that doesn't happen in the workplace.

I'm thinking about that time Guy and I were negotiating on the top of the chip pile. By rights Guy should have sent me packing. But he didn't. I asked him for my raise. "How much do you want?" he finally hollered over the clanging of conveyors and whining saws. "As much as the rest of the crew," I hollered back. Guy stopped shovelling.

"OK," he said. "OK. But you got to promise me one thing."

"What?" I said, sensing a victory.

"Quit wearing your shirt inside out."

DO ANIMALS

HAVE FUN?

My father and I were burning brush recently at his place in
the Cowichan Valley. It was near lunch and we were standing around poking the fire when two ravens flew over, spiralling and
flipping upside down. "Look at that," said Dad, squinting through
the smoke, "someone's having a good time." I said the ravens' behav-
ior reminded me of the way otters zip down mud slides. Dad said it
reminded him of what the cows used to do when he was a kid.

The cows were on my grandfather's farm in Ontario. It was
Dad's job to milk them. This was a peaceful task—with the obligatory
barn cats and the drum of warm milk in the milk pail—except for
the inclination of the cows to squish whoever was tending them.
They did this by leaning, slowly and with groans of contentment,
pressing the milker against the wall. A farm kid weighs eighty to
ninety pounds. A milk cow weighs eight hundred pounds. The

satisfaction for the cow, as Dad is fond of putting it, must have been similar to that of Bobby Hull when he greased some tiny centre against the boards.

The cows and Bobby Hull are part of an annual conversation Dad and I have regarding animal behaviour. This conversation pits the two of us against a familiar figure in our family conversations, a fictitious idiot, usually an academic of some sort, who takes the opposite side from the one we're on. In this case, the expert claims all animal behaviour can be explained in terms of survival; Dad and I say animals just like to have fun.

The cows are Exhibit A in our case. Exhibit B is dogs. Some years ago, Dad and I were in a pickup, hurtling down a nowhere section of highway west of Dawson Creek. About ten miles from our farm, we spotted something far ahead on the road. As we neared the something, we saw it was an animal. Then that it was a dog. Then that it was our dog Colonel, ten miles from home and heading out, tail wagging. Dad didn't believe in interference, so he didn't even slow the car. In the moment we flashed by—and I recall this clearly—I saw that dog smile at me. Not a smirk, not a simper, but a full-blown teethy smile. He was happy.

Over the years Colonel was to provide ample evidence that animals can have fun. Many of these stories get regurgitated during our annual discussion—one year the story about his eating a hundred and five T-bone steaks, the next year the one about chasing the piglets. But the story never omitted is the one about the squirrels. It proves my dad's other theory: animals are capable of fun because they are capable of sorrow.

Colonel always wanted to catch a squirrel. Part of this was instinct, part was the fact they made him feel like a goof. They did this by darting in front of his nose, then dashing up a fence or barn where they'd chatter and throw pine cones at him.

For the first five years of his life, Colonel was unsuccessful in his attempts to get a squirrel. Then, one late winter morning, he nailed one. Exactly how he did this remains a mystery, but Dad and I know he did it because we were there. We were in the yard readying the seeder for the upcoming season. "Look what Colonel's got," Dad said. There was the dog, marching toward us, flailing squirrel gripped firmly between his teeth. He was smiling. And as he got closer the smile got bigger and bigger until … until it was what I can only describe as a laugh. He was laughing. As it turned out, the squirrel was laughing too, because when Colonel's mouth opened the squirrel shot out and scaled a nearby pole where it and its buddies scolded Colonel for being a double loser: a dog and a goof.

Poor Colonel. His face dropped, his tail hung low. Dad and I bit our lips as we watched him pass, lest we burst out laughing.

"Colonel's sad," I said.

"I know," said Dad, "I know. That's what you get for having too much fun."

CHEKHOV'S
WHEELBARROW

January is always tough for those of us who make our living in
the country. The bottom of the firewood market sinks away
and there's little in the way of gardening or fencing work. It's a slow
time spent poking the fire and staring out the window.

Several years ago my nephew, who was also living and working in the country, came up with a good January project. Rob had
worked on an estate during the fall and noticed the landlord using a
homemade device for increasing the capacity of his wheelbarrow. It
was a rectangular affair of plywood that inserted into the barrow,
ideal for leaves, peat, etc. Perhaps it could be patented, Rob said to
me one day after New Year's. The potential was limitless.

I should say something about Rob. He is slim, large of nose,
and has a stare as intense as a kestrel. Since he was old enough to roll
coins he's been set on one thing: getting, as he puts it, stinking rich.

At fifteen he'd started his own gardening outfit, and at sixteen cornered the market on burl clocks in south Duncan. Now, at nineteen, he had his sights on something bigger.

I happen to have a head for business myself. As soon as I heard Rob's plan for the wheelbarrow I suggested what he needed was a partner. Patenting was going to take expertise, I said, reminding him I'd got a B-plus in drafting. Can't patent without a blueprint. I'd also taken bookkeeping in school—with less success, but I knew about chequing accounts and the like.

Rob was resistant to my way of thinking until I reminded him he'd been using my spare chain saw for the last year and the rent on that was still to be decided. So we shook hands and our enterprise was launched.

The Russian writer Anton Chekhov once wrote a story about a poor rural couple who buy a lottery ticket. The couple start to chat about what might happen if they win. She wants to give some to her family; he wants to give more to his family. Before long they're engaged in a hissing argument—about money they haven't even won.

That story now seems like a blueprint of sorts for what happened to Rob and me—except our rift began before any money talk. I suggested we consummate the partnership of Tom and Rob, or T & R, over a burger and beer. Rob agreed on the burger and beer part, but said R & T had a much more corporate ring than T & R, which he claimed sounded like a small-town floor covering outfit. I disagreed, and when we arrived at the nearby Oak and Carriage pub we set to designing company logos on paper napkins to prove our respective points.

Burgers and beer came and went, and talk of logos gave way to talk of money. We were speculating what we might do if, for example, we made $4 million off the patented wheelbarrow insert. Each member of our family could get $100,000 and we'd still have lots. Then I thought of a problem. What about my sister, Rob's mother? Would her $100,000 come out of Rob's share, or mine? I said she was his mother, he should give it. He said otherwise, and we proceeded to reenact Chekhov, complete with hissing, right there in the Oak and Carriage.

The whole thing could have degenerated into blows, but that's not how our family resolves disputes. Instead we departed the pub in separate taxis, both headed the same way.

I can wrap up the story of our enterprise painfully briefly. We got our act together enough to send a letter to some patent lawyers in Vancouver and included a sketch of our proposal. Two weeks after we sent it we got all our stuff back. It came to Rob's address. He brought the package to my place. It included a letter that said, in the way only lawyers can say it, that we were a couple of dimwit knobs, and might as well try patenting a sneeze. They even included the name and address of another law firm in Vancouver, should we have any more brilliant ideas.

"Well," I said, "so much for Rob and Tom Enterprises."

Rob flashed a raptor-like glance. "Don't you mean so much for Tom and Rob Enterprises?"

CHIMNEY FIRES AS
CHRISTMAS TRADITION

W e've had our first chimney fire of the winter. A gnarly chunk
of arbutus wedged in the woodstove so the door wouldn't
shut. The arbutus ignited, then the creosote in the flue, and within
minutes the stove was hyperventilating. *Woof,* it went, *woof, woof,*
like the bark of a basset hound, until it burnt itself out.

That fire, in my mind, was a fine omen. Old-timers believe
bluejays in October signal a cold winter; I believe chimney fires in
December signal a good Christmas.

Take that chimney fire at our farmhouse in 1968. It was a
week before Christmas. There were five feet of snow, yet I couldn't
get my older brothers to do any tobogganing. They were too busy
inside, reading *Hot Rod* magazine. Then the chimney took off.
Everyone scrambled outside, a ladder was run against the roof and
Dad hiked up and dumped rock salt into the flue. That killed the

fire. And now that my brothers were outside, they turned their attention to my toboggan run. Shovels were produced, as were kettles of warm water. Water was poured on the renovated turns and jumps, and we passed the rest of the day descending a bobsled track. After Christmas my brothers remembered they were too old to be having fun, and returned to *Hot Rod* magazine.

Then there was the chimney fire at my parents' place in Duncan. It was Christmas Day, circa 1978. We had finished opening our presents and were wallowing through that difficult time between the last gift and the first devilled egg. Dad escaped the house by going out to get mixer, and as he backed out the drive, he noticed a seven-foot flame venting from the chimney. Up the roof he went. As it happened, a few of his friends were heading out for mixer too and, seeing the beacon of flames from the chimney, stopped in.

I think Dad and his friends got the same satisfaction from that chimney fire as Mom had from Revered Kerr's mass at St. John's the night before. The rest of the day was a rare, peaceful bliss.

And then there was the chimney fire at the rented house in Duncan. This was just six years ago, before I met Lorna. It was Christmas Eve, and a bunch of us single guys were attempting to do the Christmas Eve thing away from our families. Potato chips and Cheezies were poured into bowls, and a relatively sedimentless batch of homemade beer was uncapped. Steve, who was the most family-minded, had decreed that Charles Dickens's *A Christmas Carol*, the one with Alastair Sim, had to be on TV. For mood, he said.

Everyone was busy wrapping presents. Somehow we failed to notice when a pile of oil-soaked rags was stuffed into the woodstove. There was a *woof*, then a sound like a jet. The stove turned an ominous orange. Someone said it didn't look right, but Steve said the glow only added to the mood.

Minutes later there was a knock at the door. In came a big man dressed in a red suit, a firefighter suit. He was the fire chief. The chief was followed by seven other firefighters, members of the Duncan Volunteer Fire Department. It was OK to burn the house, the chief declared, but not OK to burn a neighbour's house, which might very well happen if the old shack we were in ignited. He looked very serious, until he spotted the TV.

"Hey, is that the one with Alastair Sim?" he said.

"Yeah," said Steve, who was still glued to the set. He wasn't about to fracture the seasonal mood for something so trifling as a chimney fire.

"I haven't seen this for years," said the chief, perching, boots and all, on a stool. The chief waved his crew off to do their thing with the stove and the chimney, while he and Steve discussed the virtues of classic films.

It took the firefighters ten minutes to calm the stove. They headed out the door with the chief following reluctantly.

"Excuse me," one of my buddies said to them, "but how did you know we had a chimney fire?"

"Oh. A lady phoned," said the chief. "She was heading home from mass and saw flames. You might want to thank her sometime. Name's Mrs. Henry.

"Nice to meet you. Oh, and Merry Christmas."

SPRING

WHEN A TREE FALLS

L ife in the country is often defined by what it isn't. It isn't hectic, crime-ridden, smog-filled; it isn't, or at least it's not supposed to be, complicated by debates on trends: the '80s look, the '90s tone.

Why, then, I have been asking myself, is this community embroiled in a highly theoretical debate about a single tree?

The tree, a balsam, is three miles due east of my house. Four feet through, one hundred and fifty feet high. It grew on property belonging to Wayne. During a recent windstorm it blew over onto property belonging to Ivan and a right-of-way belonging to the municipality.

For Ivan, who is alleged to have Greenpeace affiliations, the standing tree had represented a potential home for the marbled murrelet, or some such enviro-critter. But the moment the tree went over, it was transformed into an economic unit: Ivan saw logging megabucks. For Wayne, the fallen tree represented next year's firewood.

Question is, who gets the tree?

Both men want it. Both have enlisted so many friends and neighbours in support of their respective cases that the tree has superseded horse trails as the community's preeminent pound-the-table, go-red-in-the-face issue.

The municipality doesn't want the tree, but has told both landowners not to touch it before the matter is properly resolved, or they'll face the consequences.

That effectively puts the kibosh on the most effective method of resolving disputes over trees. Namely, nipping in with a saw and cutting it up before anyone figures out what's going on. Two fellows from around here made good money doing something similar on Crown land. They would go in with a five-dollar firewood permit, then turn left when they were supposed to turn right. Deep in the woods, they'd fall and buck a first-growth cedar into shake blocks. They'd pack the blocks, worth six hundred dollars a cord, into the truck and envelop them with a layer of alder, worth a hundred and twenty dollars a cord. That was a precaution, in case a nosy forester happened by. There was so much money in the deal they could afford to sweep and vacuum the area where they'd worked.

Their mistake was showing up in a new Ford 4x4. Everybody knows woodcutters can't afford good trucks. A watchman decided to have a closer look. He saw the Hoover, and the wood thieves got a chance to think about their errors in the crowbar hotel.

Wayne's claim to the infamous tree is based on the notion of First Causes. The tree grew from his land, nourished on his nutrients, and thus belongs to him. He wavered briefly when a friend pointed out that by such reasoning, Wayne might be held responsible for his children, the eldest of which is up on a drunk driving charge. But Wayne responded that the kid was rotten and the tree was not, so the analogy didn't stand.

Ivan's argument is even more tenuous. Ivan admits the tree originated from Wayne's land but, as he points out, so does water in a stream that runs through the two properties. The water doesn't belong to anyone. Furthermore, says Ivan, the tree grew with a lean. It existed in air above his land for years and was predestined to land on his property.

And so it's gone, back and forth, the two men and their supporters arguing to no resolution.

Three days ago, someone suggested a neat solution. Both men have bulldozers. Why not hook them up and pull? Strongest machine wins. It would have kept with the philosophical nature of our debate, bearing close resemblance to the story about the two thinkers who argue so vigorously over a baby they pull it in half.

Yesterday, however, we discovered the bulldozer solution was academic. So were all the reasoned arguments for who should get the log. While Wayne and Ivan were debating, someone nipped in and solved the problem for them, and got a couple cords of firewood to boot.

Another Thing
About Lunch

*I*n the bay in front of our home, between the log booms and
Granny's Beach, there is a small floating shack. It sits on two big
cedars and swings freely at the end of a length of wire rope spiked to
a piling. The shack itself is rectangular and sided with shingles. It is
unremarkable, except for the large section of roof that overhangs the
plank porch. This overhang looks like a baseball cap pulled low; I
never look at the shack without thinking it's having a really good
snooze.

The shack is the lunchroom for those of us on the boom
crew. It's also dry storage for six hundred feet of two-inch tow line,
hundreds of feet of smaller line, life vests, pike poles, peavies, shack-
les, caulk boots and a mangled blue crab trap.

I found that crab trap on Saturday while working on a boom.
It was tangled in a bundle of logs. "What do you want me to do with

this thing?" I asked Dave after I hauled it aboard the boat. I might as well have asked what to do with a cold beer on a hot day. "Put it in the lunchroom," he said. "What else?"

There's something appealing about a place where you have all this stuff going on: ropes and sandwiches and crab traps. A practical filthiness that you don't find in restaurants, or even at home. My home is no more or less messy than most, yet when I have lunch, I fret over unwashed dishes, dirty windows, dehydrated plants. The demands of home economics prohibit true indolence. In the lunchroom, there is none of that. It is a place where you go to do one thing: eat your lunch. And if you feel like tipping the ash from your cigarette on your pants and rubbing it in, fine.

When I first started working on the booms two years ago, there was a cup of something—coffee with a piece of apple in it, perhaps—on the table. The cup is still there now, though the contents have metamorphosed. Nobody is concerned about it, and nobody cares that nobody is concerned.

Another thing about lunchrooms. They are peaceful. Homes, at best, are safe places and places to grow in, but they are not peaceful. There are too many different ages and sexes, with too many interests, to be so placid. Lunchrooms, on the other hand, are often uni-sexual; men only. And the men are roughly the same age, with the same qualities. They work at the same job—in my case, with logs—so work backgrounds every conversation. It's as if we all use the same software.

I worked at a place once with such a pleasant lunchroom that an employee actually wanted to move in. This was at a sawmill in Chemainus. The lunchroom was an early '60s trailer, one that came factory direct with a divan and dirty pictures on the walls. It was homey in the same way that Spam straight from the can is homey. Salty. Easy to squish.

While I was working there, Jimmy, the loader operator, a

small man with an oversized head, broke up with his wife. First he moved the components from his supersonic stereo into the lunch trailer so she wouldn't get them. Then he asked if he might bunk down. Just for a few nights. OK, said the boss.

Some time later Jimmy was driving by the trailer with a load of logs when he happened to sneeze. A hemlock sawlog fell from the grapple onto the trailer, smashing one corner to smithereens. At lunch, the crew inspected the damage—the burst ribbing, the gaping hole in the roof—and wondered aloud if this would force Jimmy into a reconciliation. But Jimmy, whose comfy chair was buckled, simply hoisted off the broken pieces of tin, swept away the dust and unwrapped a store-bought sandwich.

"Ah, let's see here," he purred.

The lunchroom was a lunchroom, no matter what.

"It sure beats being cooped up in the old house," Jimmy said.

DUMB PETS

When my family talks about dumb pets—that is, pets that are stupid—we talk about our black lab, Colonel. There are many examples of Colonel's dumbness: repeat encounters with porcupines, bears and four-hundred-pound sows. All made deep impressions everywhere but his brain.

When winter temperatures on our farm dipped to twenty or more below, Colonel, who was an outdoor dog, was allowed indoors. He'd be curled in front of the oil heater while my brothers and I lounged about reading or playing cards. Then, slowly, an oily sulphur smell would envelop the room. The dog had farted. We'd laugh, of course, because that's what brothers do when dogs fart. Colonel treated it more seriously and would go to the door and growl menacingly, warning us something dangerous and smelly was lurking outside. Then *we'd* have to pat him and say "That's OK, boy, that's OK," and settle him down.

Colonel was not the only less-than-bright pet my family has had. No Lassies for us, or that dog of Farley Mowat's. Remember the Dog Who Wouldn't Be, and how it could operate an overhead projector and taught Farley to ride his CCM Red Rider? Or was it the other way around?

I have a friend who clips an outdoors column from the *Guardian*, in which amazing pet feats are recounted: dogs that hiked the Urals, cats who crossed four provinces to find their owners. Last week I saw one about a terrier that was in a car wreck on a remote road in Scotland. It survived, then led rescuers to the crash site just in time to save the injured driver.

Colonel couldn't have done that. The one time he had the chance to do something heroic, he flopped. My brother Guy was ploughing a field late one evening and got stuck. He tried to back up, which itself was a dumb thing to do—but this is about pets, not brothers—and the plough jackknifed and pinned Guy to the tractor. Colonel was nearby, and Guy, who was shaken but not injured, shouted for him. "Go home, Colonel. Get help!" (Everyone sounds like Lorne Greene when they talk seriously to their pets.)

Colonel went home all right, and he snuck up to my brother's room and went to sleep on his bed. I guess he figured there was a vacancy. It wasn't until midnight that Dad realized something was wrong and rescued Guy.

After Colonel came a roster of dumb pets, including Mrs. McLeod, a cat terrified of her own reflection, and Henry. Henry is my nephew's poodle mongrel. He's about the size of a case of beer, and likes rocks about half that size, which, somehow, he picks up in his mouth. When Henry tries to walk with one of the heavy loads, his hind legs come off the ground, spinning, and his snout slowly tips forward until—*crunch*. My nephew's reaction is similar to a parent whose kid just flunked their Orange Jellyfish swim class for the fourth time. Lots of love, but a hint, too, of wishful thinking.

I'm going to tell one more story about dumb pets, involving my brother Paul and his dog Hippo. Paul and Hippo lived together in a subdivision in Whitehorse. Not long after Paul got Hippo, as a pup, we began to get concerned letters. The dog was too much, Paul said. Uncontrollable. An idiot. Nothing worked, not even obedience classes. Just how bad the dog was I discovered when I went north for a visit. When mowing the lawn or playing ball, the dog—black lab-ish, with a tail like a question mark—would exit normal behaviour and enter a hyper mode. He'd get low to the ground and tear, tear around, in a wild pattern. Everyone would stop what they were doing and watch the dog go round and round until finally he'd shoot out of the yard, like a rocket slingshotting out of a planet's pull. Into deep neighbourhood. We'd go inside and wait. Two, three hours later Hippo would show up, wondering where everyone had gone and why we weren't playing any more.

Not long ago, we received a call from Paul. Hippo was gone. For good.

"Run away?" I asked.

"No."

"Sent to the pound?"

"No."

"What happened?"

"Found a place in the country for him," said Paul. "It's the only place for idiots like that."

THE MAJOR

*L*ong before we moved to this property, an interesting and wizened man ran the place. His name was Russell, but I'm told he was known as "the Major," and that's how I think of him.

I never met the Major—he died five years before we moved here. But I run into him when I'm gardening or cutting wood: he lurks in ivy-laden rock walls that I've uncovered, and he's there on the narrow boardwalk he built, the one my daughter and I use to get from the bluff to Granny's Beach. He's even in the tobacco cans of salvaged nails in our garage. He pounded each nail straight, and sorted them into the proper tins as if he knew we were going to need them.

A ghost? No. The Major doesn't appear as a wavy apparition—I'm too literal-minded to believe my eyes if I saw a real ghost anyway—but rather as a tangible precedent. It's as if he endures in the work he did here, and his efforts have set a tone I'm obliged to carry on. I think of him as the good neighbour, whose tended lawn and lush rhodos set the standard for the entire street.

Over the years and on other farms, I've lived in the shadow of a few characters like the Major. On our family farm in the 1960s, for instance, we were rarely without the company of an aging sallow-faced pioneer named Henry Bagney. Henry Bagney was the previous owner of the farm who, after selling out, had gone first to an apartment in Dawson Creek, then to his Maker. We had one photo of him. He was at the edge of a large clearing, pulling over poplars with a team of shaggy, swaybacked workhorses. He cleared the whole farm that way, day after sweaty day, transforming forest to field. We had that farm for five years, and every day the spirit of Henry Bagney watched over us, nodding in approval when we got up early and worked hard, shaking his head in despair when we opted for frivolities like the occasional afternoon barbecue.

Another time, when a buddy and I were renting a shack and twenty acres, we were haunted by the spirit of a shrubby dope dealer. He'd lived on the property years before. Apparently he was a flop at growing pot: we found the remains of a half-built greenhouse in the bush, including electrical wire strung on trees for heat lamps. My friend and I had hopes for that place. We were going to raise bedding plants and chickens, we were going to cut wood from the woodlot. We worked hard, but each project sloughed in on itself. We later decided the old dealer had cast a flunk-out pall on the place, and we took a house in town.

I have never seen evidence that the Major failed to complete a single job. I have also never seen a picture of him. I have formed a picture, by noting the differences between his son, who is my landlord, and the Major's widow, who I occasionally work for. A hereditary subtraction: son minus the mother equals the father.

The Major was, I imagine, a slight man, with distinctive eyes and a high, handsome brow. He was tough, in the way that skinny British guys are tough. I know he swam every day of the year in the bay, bare-assed, and followed this with a cold shower. I'm sure he must have been purple year round.

About the Major's character I know slightly more. He was a voracious reader. He made bad wine and drank one glass each day, just before dinner. He also raised chickens, salvaged logs, gardened vigorously. He was intensely interested in everything, which seems like the most valuable attribute for living in the country.

Our place is a nearly ideal mix of farm, forest and water. It's good to have someone like the Major standing by, to show us how to use it.

"Broker"

Whenever our car coughs or splutters, as it's been doing lately, I think of my friend Mike. Mike is my car broker. Actually he's a potato farmer who doubles as a commercial fisherman, but I call him a broker because over the years he's landed me some remarkable deals on cars.

The first vehicle Mike helped me purchase—and the one where he demonstrated his bargaining skills—was a 1968 station wagon called a Vista Cruiser. It belonged to a red-faced old fellow off Drinkwater Road, north of Duncan. Walt, as he introduced himself when I dropped in, said he was selling the car because his kids were finally out of the house. He'd used it for trips to Disneyland but now did his travelling in front of the TV. The price was six hundred dollars—firm. I rounded up Mike a day later and returned to dicker.

Dickering has never been my family's strength, as I had seen many times when my dad went to buy livestock. "That will be fifty dollars for that sow, Bill." "I'll give you forty dollars." "No, fifty." "Well, OK then," and Dad would fork out the fifty bucks.

Mike, on the other hand, liked dealing. As he says, anyone who has picked potatoes for a living has to be frugal.

I've always associated bargaining with lively banter, offer and counter offer. Not Mike. Mikes uses silence. Witness what happened at old Walt's. After a cursory look at the Cruiser, Mike took up a position just off the front fender. There he stood hunkered in his hockey jacket, eyes unblinking, cigarette pinched dead centre of his mouth. Time slowed to a geologic scale. Even the second hand on my wrist watch shuffled.

I don't know who suffered more, the seller or me. I come from a family that regards silence the same way a graffiti artist regards a subway wall—as a wasted opportunity. I fiddled and twitched until Mike, reptile-like, gave me a glance to stop.

Mike's bargaining technique took only slightly longer to get hold of Walt. At first he bustled around the car, pointing out bits of work he'd done: a touchup on the rear fender, new weather stripping, a recent oil change. Gradually, though, his conversation petered out and he was reduced to paring his fingernails with a jackknife and saying, "Yep, she's a good old car, all right," and "You can't beat a Chev."

I was reminded of what my mom used to do when she was mad at one of us kids. Like the time my brother Guy accidentally ran the fourteen-foot International Harvester chisel plough through Mom's rhubarb patch. Mom simply clammed up. Household conversation was reduced to a minimum, as were her pork chop dinners, which were normally succulent affairs with mushrooms and onions. Dry meat and a boiled potato was all we got, with a curt thin-lipped announcement that there was no dessert. It was too much. If Guy hadn't offered to restore the rhubarb on his own, we would have done it for him, just to get some noise happening.

The same thing happened with Walt and the car. After what seemed like hours of silence, he relented and started to do the bargaining for us. "Well," he said, "it does have a lot of miles; I guess I could go down to four-fifty." A few minutes later he observed the tires were balding, and four hundred might be a more appropriate price. Then he remembered the transmission leaked a little and went to three seventy-five. On it went until he suggested we'd be doing him a heck of a favour if we'd take the car off his hands for two hundred bucks.

"OK," said Mike, and produced from his jacket pocket transfer papers and pen, cap already off.

I drove the Vista Cruiser home that day and Mike followed in his truck. We almost made it into my driveway when steam erupted from under the hood. A heater hose had ruptured. "Why that old bugger," I said, "he told me this car used to make it down to Disneyland and back."

"That was in a five-hundred-dollar car," said Mike. "The car you're driving isn't worth half that."

UNTARNISHED
LABOURS

*L*ast Thursday I worked seven hours picking rocks from a farmer's field. I took a large iron bar and methodically walked back and forth over twenty acres, prying stones loose and tossing them into small piles. Then I drove the farmer's flatdeck around the field, collecting the piles, and dumped them in a ditch. By the time I was done I was hungry, my nose was clogged with dirt clinkers and my back hurt. But there was not one rock in that field larger than my fist.

Of all the labouring work I do, or have done, rock picking has to be the most nakedly simple. It makes logging, with all its machinery and attendant dangers, seem impossibly complex by comparison. Even wood cutting requires some attention. There is the chain saw to deal with, and different woods must be split in different ways. With rock picking, though, your brain can be as inert as the material you're working with. You grunt the iron bar under a rock, you heave it onto a pile. Clang, clack, iron and stone, hour after hour.

I like this kind of work. It is so elemental that there is nothing to complain about. No photocopier to jam, no computer program to crash, no phone to be busy. It's entirely up to you to decide whether to hate or enjoy what you are doing.

One of my favourite parts of rock picking is the food. When I'm doing less strenuous jobs I watch what I eat. Not too many eggs, low-fat milk. When I pick rocks, all that goes out the window. My thinking is that hard work does to fat and cholesterol what a hot fire does to PCBs and plastic: it reduces them to their original and harmless elements. At eleven-thirty, I got a craving for sticky buns and coffee with cream. I zipped down to the sticky bun store and bought a bucket of coffee and six buns and ate them all at once, with butter and without regret. Where all that dough and sugar went I'm not sure, but by three in the afternoon I was hungry again.

And picking rocks is harmless. Every other job I work at gives me niggling doubts about its worth. I enjoy falling trees, for example, and know wood is used for useful things. Still, I can't help thinking at the end of the day that the world would be a better place if I had just stayed in bed.

Even gardening is not guilt-free. I wonder sometimes if the feeble, weak-kneed species of hybrids we are creating wouldn't be better off left to compete on their own. A clean field seems to me a natural thing.

I was picking rocks in someone else's field. It has been suggested to me that picking rocks would be even more satisfying were the field my own, that I would be improving my own land for my own benefit. I know what they are saying, but I disagree. There is something honourable about doing good, simple work for someone else. Joseph Conrad once said the best part of being a sailor was that you knew you were doing good work for the sake of doing it well, not because you owned the ship. A sailor's labours weren't tarnished by the pride of ownership.

I like that. The field where I picked rocks is beside the road into town. I'll enjoy driving past it for years to come.

POINT OF
ORDER

When I moved to the country I vowed to never, ever, join an organization, club or group. I wanted nothing to do with people who get together and say things like "point of order," or drink coffee from urns. The pettiness that goes along with organizations seemed to me antithetical to the do-as-you-please of rural life.

Then, about this time last year, we signed up our daughter for preschool. The preschool is a co-op; parental involvement is mandatory. Faced with a choice between having my kid become a recluse or breaking a vow, I chose the latter, but with the same noisy reluctance Lily reserves for cold cabbage.

My hesitation was largely the result of a nasty experience I had several years ago, when I was living in the Cowichan Valley. I decided to join a small environmental group whose stated purpose was to preserve local agricultural land—your classic think global, act local campaign. The group was new; I think I attended their second meeting. The meeting occurred in, of all places, a subdivision home built on hay fields. The host was a waxy-faced high school counsellor who greeted me with a funny handshake. He convened the meeting by strumming a guitar. To get us into the right head space, he said.

First on the agenda was an ad campaign. What was second I never did find out, because the meeting collapsed before we got that far. The trouble with the ad campaign was that someone suggested we buy several sheets of plywood for signs. "Whoa," said another member, almost spilling her peppermint tea. "Plywood comes from the forest. Remember what we stand for?" Someone else suggested we use a synthetic material, but that was shot down because it was made from petroleum. As the disagreement heated, our waxy-faced host strummed ever more vigorously on his guitar, searching for the elusive head space. Another person proposed a middle ground—buying particle board—but not before shouting, "I can't hear anything."

It seemed to me a classic case of thinking global, acting yokel. I slipped away, vowing to never waste my time again.

Until, that is, the preschool came along. If you think I'm going to do an about-face and say warm gooey things about the preschool, or any other rural organization, you're wrong. They still feature pettiness and a share of back stabbing. But they do accomplish things, in their own manner. And more important, they are a place to get out and meet people. This is a point about organizations I think is too often lost in the rush of business.

The success of organizations, at least rural ones, is directly related to their surroundings. Our preschool meetings take place in the preschool building, actually a sagging church hall. The meetings take place at night. When you pull up in front of the hall, or drive by, or maybe even fly overhead, an oversensitive light winks on. "Come on in," it says. Inside, the hall is heated by a furnace that won't go off. It gets very hot. People who arrive brisk and determined with agenda soon begin to shed their clothes and fan themselves slowly with kiddies' art work. The heat makes thoughts wander, and it is not uncommon to see a father eyeing a particularly bold Lego structure, thinking how he might do better.

Occasionally, while sipping urn-made coffee and daydreaming at meetings, it occurs to me that our provincial and federal governments might do well to hold session in such places, where the Brio trains and the Playmobiles would distract them from pettiness, where the winking light would let them know they are always welcome, and where nothing is out of reach.

CEE PEE'S
TREES

I am never more aware of the forest surrounding our cabin than I am in April. At night I'm kept awake by westerlies that tear the tops off balsams. Mornings, I'm drawn to the unfurling broadleaf maple, which buzzes with hummingbirds. In the late afternoons I curse the firs casting long shadows over our vegetable garden.

Trees, trees, trees. For all my attempts at civilization, I am still, at heart, a forest dweller.

It's impossible for me to think of trees without thinking of C.P. Lyons. Lyons—or, as he is known affectionately in this house, Ol' Cee Pee—is the author of *Trees, Shrubs & Flowers to Know in BC.* Since it was first issued in 1952, the book has become a standard on cabin bookshelves. My copy occupies a place of honour near the back door, where I can reach it quickly without taking off my boots.

In his own way, Cee Pee has done for the province's trees

what William Faulkner did for small-town Mississippi, or what Jack Hodgins has done for Vancouver Island. He's given them character, temperament and mood. According to Cee Pee, hemlock tops don't merely droop, they droop "gracefully"; branches of the Sitka spruce are not horizontal, but "strongly out-thrust." His sentences are clear, like the tang of freshly split cedar. This is not the language of a desk-bound, pencil-necked gink; this is the language of a robust outdoors-man with big thighs. A man who delights in nature and is not afraid to say so. A biographical note on the back cover says that Cee Pee learned much of what he knows about nature while playing hooky. To read his descriptions is to share in the thrill of trading the math book for a backpack and taking off for the day.

Beside each of Cee Pee's written entries is an accompanying sketch of a tree. Sometimes these sketches include the figure of a man. Cee Pee inserted the drawings for perspective and scale, but for those of us who consult the book regularly (and there are many), the sketch man has come to represent something more. Just the presence of a man changes the book. Cee Pee could have used a yardstick, or a car, and the effect would have been antiseptic. But a man suggests company, fellowship.

Nor is this any ordinary man. He is dressed in heavy over-jacket, tie and hat. The hat has a flat brim and is worn at an angle that suggests it has been worn that way many times. The man's gaze is straight and honest. He seems comfortable in the woods, although less so under the towering pine on page 18 than he does under the red alder on page 40.

Much has been made of this man—in print and among my friends. One friend, who has a degree in English, says the figure is clearly autobiographical. Cee Pee, she says, is obviously a shy, retiring man. Why else would he sketch the man behind the Hairy Manzanita? Another friend, an ardent environmentalist, attributes more serious meaning to the sketch man. According to this friend, he represents the triumph of western imperialism over nature. We need to have a human figure before nature—even a red alder—has any meaning.

But all that is too sophisticated for me. I know who the man is in Cee Pee's book. Always have. He's Cee Pee's teacher, looking for Cee Pee, who's skipped out, again.

PLENTY

Frank and I share a garden. Her good soil, my strong back; we go fifty-fifty on the seeds and the produce.

Normally, Frank's manner on the phone is taciturn, especially on my answering machine. "Hi Tom. Frank here. The deer got in and ate all the kale. Thought I'd let you know. Bye."

Not her most recent call. Enthusiasm bolted out of the machine, like a radish in chicken manure. "Tom," she said. "The seeds are in from Ontario! Think we can get the cauliflower started right away? Bye. Oh. P.S. I still think you're crazy to try celery. Anyway, see you soon."

Around here, spring may be dated officially from the moment seeds arrive. Ankle-deep snow outside, ducks frozen in the pond, it doesn't matter. When that box pops out of the mailbox, it's spring. It's a part of the seasons, like winter solstice, or the equinox.

I have mixed emotions about this. Going through a box of seeds you ordered months ago is a bit like leafing through your journal. It's embarrassing. Crops that seemed like a great idea back in December, when I stayed up late at the kitchen table making plans for this year's garden, now seem really stupid. Like popcorn. My dad used to grow popcorn. Twenty acres of it. This was in 1949, on his farm in Ontario. Last December I thought it would be cool if I grew some too, to bridge the decades with him.

Now, I wonder where my mind was. I mean, at one time Dad had some shares in a VSE dud called Amalgamated Doorknob, too, but I wouldn't dream of rebonding through penny stocks.

Two kinds of cabbage? Red *and* green? Last year we ended up with forty mature cabbages at one time. My appetite for sauerkraut is finite, but my hopes I'd find a useful purpose for all these heads was infinite. So they sat in the ground, rotting. A rotting cabbage is first-class accommodation for a cabbage moth, and I expect there will be a full plague this summer. Maybe that's why I ordered so many seeds: so the bugs would have something to eat.

And then there's zucchini. I must have been overcome by doubts in December—that's the only reason I can think of for ordering zucchini. With one plant I throw the gourds away. Last year, even the food banks weren't taking squash. But with zucchini, at least you know the garden will produce something in abundance.

That's the down side of getting the seeds. The up side is that now you can take all those silly, colour-coded, graph paper plans you made at the kitchen table and throw them in the woodstove. Back in December, I swore off planting too early. Or too much. That's what amateurs do. Mature gardeners like myself are more disciplined. With Mozart in the background and a collection of soil-stained gardening tomes on a chair beside me, I drew a map of the garden. Blues indicating plants that needed to be started inside; greens indicating plants for April seeding, reds for May, and so on. On the side was a key indicating distances, ratios, volumes. The garden of my mind was to be a modest but well-tended factory, spitting out precise units of fresh produce. I was a mature agrarian, ambling around, touching leaves lovingly, maybe reciting Latin names.

Now that the seeds have come, I say to hell with that. Yesterday I stripped the crumbling plastic and dead plants out of the garden; today I'm going to rototill. Another pass over with the tiller tomorrow and in go the onions. According to my plans, they aren't supposed to go in until April, but who's going to know the difference. After that it's garlic, then spinach, maybe even zucchini. The whole package. That way Frank will have plenty to throw away, too.

THE UNCLE TIMOTHY
PRINCIPLE

The writer and farmer John Gould once framed the central dilemma of country living. Do you get up with the sun, he asked, and start wrestling with the never-ending series of chores on a farm? Or do you accept that never-ending chores are exactly that—never-ending—and snooze until mid-morning?

Gould, who farmed in New England in the 1940s, favoured getting up early. His uncle Timothy, a much older and, in my opinion, wiser man, argued the case for sleeping in. The reason you should sleep in, said Uncle Timothy, was that expenses don't start until the moment you get out of bed.

I'll vouch for that. I got out of bed early last week. The idea was to get a good start on rototilling the vegetable garden I share with Frank. Up at five-thirty, pancakes, boysenberry jam, two cups black coffee and out the door.

I arrived, only to discover the shop was locked. The rototiller was in the shop. No problem, I thought. One of the advantages of living in the country is that you know how to sneak into everyone else's barn, workshop, house, etc. But on the way through the crack in the sliding doors I laid a nice racing stripe of grease across my shirt.

Then I discovered the tire on the rototiller was flat. Again, not an insurmountable problem, especially for a guy with a truck. I'll take the rototiller to a garage. I opened the truck canopy, placed two sturdy planks for a ramp, and started the rototiller. Up the ramp it went, up and up and up, until the gas tank on top of the rototiller popped like a periscope through the rear canopy window of the truck, sending glass flying.

By this time it was seven-thirty. Usually I'd just be getting out of bed. Today I was outside, in a greasy shirt, picking glass out of my hair. Either way, the garden wasn't rototilled. Only by getting up early had I succeeded in putting myself seventy-five dollars in the hole—that being the price of a new rear window. Proof, once again, of the overwhelming power of the Uncle Timothy Principle.

But the morning wasn't over. I zipped home, fetched Lily and headed for the local feed store for chicken pellets.

Lily and I usually do our feed store business in the after-noons, and we always talk with the same nice lady behind the counter. She lets Lily feed the hamsters and gerbils. On this morning, however, there was a man behind the counter. He had on one of those fringed black vests, the kind former bikers sell at the Coombs Bluegrass Festival.

We'd been in the store a few minutes, and I was looking at cowboy hats, when suddenly, from the direction of the gerbils, comes a banshee, *Daaaad!* A moment later Lily came tearing down the aisle, sobbing. Behind her marched Mr. Fringe, clutching two handfuls of tiny biscuits. It seems Lily had thoughtlessly mixed gerbil food with hamster food, and this fellow was worried about the two alchemically combining and blowing the feed store sky high. Or some such crap. So he had yanked the food out of her hand and given her stern words.

I wish I could report that I did something brave at this point, like chain saw his desk in half. But I just took my sobbing daughter and did the only thing you can do with a sobbing daughter at that time of the morning. We went to the ice cream store and had doubles.

Later, on the way home, Lily fretted about why the feed store man was so crabby. Maybe he was sick, she said. Or sad. Or he didn't want to share. That one she could get her head around. Between her ponderings I tallied the morning's expenses. Window, shirt, loss of a local source of feed, ice cream—about a hundred and twenty bucks, by my figuring.

Finally, at the top of our drive, Lily announced her diagnosis of the badly behaved feed store man. "Dad, sometimes when I get up too early? And you say I have to take a nap? Maybe that crabby guy needs a nap, too," she said.

Uncle Timothy would approve, I think, since he figured the more time sleeping, the fewer expenses incurred. Tomorrow, I will try the new regime: rise late, nap often, and try to balance the books.

UNCLE PAUL'S
OUTHOUSE

This spring Lorna and I are fixing up a clapboard shack that is about fifty feet back in the bush from our cabin. By fix up I mean we have swept off a layer of topsoil from the roof of hand-split cedar shakes, and we will prop up the corners of the porch, which sag at both ends. The porch is so rotten it should really have come off. But I said, "What the heck, I'll do it next year."

There's always a temptation to completely overhaul these kinds of structures, to repanel and mount flyfishing rods on the wall so they resemble something out of a glossy magazine, but I know better.

I had an uncle—he's dead three years now—who couldn't resist the urge to fix things up. Uncle Paul lived on a small farm in the Cowichan Valley. He also had some land with several cottages near Maple Bay. In all he lorded over dozens of woodsheds, tool shops, hutches, pens, barns, boat sheds and other structures you find on rural acreages. Did a single door of his ever scrape on unoiled hinges? Did it ever drag on the floor, so you had to shoulder it open? Did a window ever jam, so it had to be pounded with the palm of your hand, then kept open with an upright beer bottle? No. Uncle Paul's farm was the platonic ideal of a farm, the type that the Wallace Hinge Company of Wallace, Wisconsin would use in an advertisement. Everything opened and closed and slid and locked in a happy, proper way.

You might think a man who maintained such high standards would be a small, measly fellow, with a multi-headed screwdriver in a back pocket and a habit of saying: "If a job's worth doing ..." You wouldn't be thinking of Uncle Paul. Uncle Paul was a large man, with a laugh like a kingfisher. He drove a Ford pickup, because the springs in the seat back of a Ford pickup would hold several dozen of his favourite beer, Silver Spring. He turned every job into a mega-project of sorts, with extension cords and skill saws and long, foul-mouthed chautauquas on what that rotten Dave Barrett and his socialist ilk were doing to the province.

I admired Uncle Paul's approach, mainly because squeaky doors and wonky windows were not uncommon in our house. We even had a toilet that flushed for two and a half months, but that's another story. The thing that changed my mind about Uncle Paul's perfectionism—and this is the reason why I'm content to leave an old shack an old shack—is what happened to his outhouse. He built this outhouse on his property in Maple Bay. The main cottage had a toilet, but it was prone to backing up when under heavy use, as it often was with his many daughters and their boyfriends, buddies, etc. So Uncle Paul decided to build an auxiliary system, in the form of an outhouse in the nearby bush. I was about fourteen at the time, and Dad and I got roped into giving him a hand.

Most outhouses sit over large, rough-hewn holes in the ground. The hole we dug was cubical, with well-defined corners and sides shorn of tree roots. And the actual building—it was the type of place where you'd write haikus about garlic and ferns. It was built of shiplap, spiked to a frame of 2x4s on a twelve-inch centre. Only native woods were used; knots and sappy bits went onto a bonfire. The topping feature was a magnificent cedar door, with a sturdy simple lock and a moon and star lovingly cut in at eye level. It was a beautiful structure, even by Uncle Paul's standards. Everyone was reluctant to use it, until the old system backed up.

All that work, and what happened? One of my cousins had a boyfriend who was a rugby player. He was also the son of a Socred MLA. He was using the outhouse one day not long after it was built, and his wallet somehow got dislodged from his pocket and went down the hole. Apparently sons of Socred MLAs value their wallets above all else, because in the fury of losing his wallet, this young man beat up my uncle's outhouse. He took it apart board by board until it was a pile of rubble. It might have been hit by a chip truck.

The whole incident is replete with lessons, some of which are too political for me to want to go into. My uncle saw it as an opportunity and built a new, albeit more modest, outhouse. As for me, I see the incident as an allegory for what happens a) when you make too much of a simple thing and b) when you allow your daughters to pick their own friends. I try to do neither.

Animal Stories

I was working at a neighbour's some time ago, turning sod and burning refuse, when I heard the long, low whine of a car backing up. It was coming in my direction—and fast. Along the straightaway, around the curve, past me on the other side of the cedar hedge and down the driveway toward my house.

Turns out the landlady, Jean, had just caught sight of a bull elk. It was grazing beside the road in a swath of blowdown. Somebody spotted an elk in East Sooke Park last year, but otherwise, sightings around here are as rare as high heels. Jean was so excited she reversed a full half mile back to fetch Lorna from our cabin. "If anybody's gonna believe this one," she explained to Lorna, "I'm gonna need a witness."

There are a couple of things that go into a good animal story. Like details. The elk sighting and Jean's driving make a good story, but not as good as the one I heard at the general store the other day. In that one, a black-tailed doe got its feet stuck in the roof of a Cortina. It kicked around so much it split the driver's nose before she could get the car stopped. A split nose is a good detail.

Fish stories can be good for the same reason—although I wouldn't be saying so if I hadn't been talking to my seventy-something neighbour the other day. I was clipping ivy when she came out to see how I was doing. We got talking and she told me about the time when every minnow in the bay formed an enormous ball and tried barrelling into the sky. The cormorants and gulls were in a feeding frenzy, and the tiny fish attempted to launch themselves into the air as a means of escape. Phyllis said, "It sounded like rain."

A good animal story needs gestures, too. And I'm not talking about sighting down a fictitious 30-30, or yarding on a make-believe fly rod. Phyllis wiggled her long fingers in the air to imitate the minnows. Jean and my wife both held their arms straight out, like preachers, to show the antler spread on their elk.

My friend Jim is a master storyteller. Jim used to log on Princess Royal Island, and claims it's home to a little double-billed bird that hates humans. "They come right at ya like this," he says, flapping hands the size of chuck steaks beside his ears. By the time the story ends you don't care whether the bird existed or not, but you're sure you've seen it yourself.

Most of all, though, a good animal story needs the right amount of heart. Last month, over coffee and Nanaimo bars at her kitchen table, Jean told me about the cougar that got hold of a lamb she'd bottle-fed from birth. The cougar ripped it apart. Jean shot the cat, but not before it grabbed another lamb. "Buried the poor things up behind the big maple," she said. Cougars are common around here and Jean hasn't wanted to raise sheep since.

The conversation was miring in sentiment.

"So what happened to the cougar?" I asked, hoping to perk things up.

Jean pointed to an oak armchair in the corner. Draped over it was the golden hide—head and tail included—of one very dead cougar.

DITCHES AND
DUMPSTERS

Every weekday during spring, Lily and I make the half-mile walk from our place up the lane to the Busy Road. Theoretically, the purpose of this walk is to check the mail, but both Lily and I have ulterior motives.

For Lily, it's a chance to throw sticks into a minuscule little stream that feeds the swamp. She's been doing this for two springs, and the resulting tangle looks as if a gang of four-inch beavers has been working overtime.

I use the mail walk as an excuse to check out the ditches. Ditches are the rural equivalent of dumpsters; if you know what to look for, and where, you can find some neat stuff. Over the years, in ditches here and elsewhere, I've found axes, shovels, 2x4s, chain saw pieces, rolls and rolls of pink surveyor's tape, plywood, jackets and hats. Especially hats. My thinking is that people must take off their hat before getting into a car or truck. They drive away and the hat spins into a ditch. I find it, slap it on my knee, and say, "Hey, Lily! Look! *Another* hat!"

There are tricks to finding stuff in a ditch, just as there are to dumpster diving. With dumpsters, unless you're hungry, you stay away from restaurants. Dumpsters near restaurants are thick with grease and mustard and mayonnaise, and anything good, like furniture or clothes, is slimy. With ditches, the choice is between those running beside straight sections of road, and those running beside curvy sections. Straight ditches are where you find the cash crops—beer bottles, pop cans, etc. The reason is (and this isn't my own thinking) that straight-aways provide drivers with a chance to roll a window down and pitch stuff out.

Curves, on the other hand, are where you find the miscellaneous treasures—lumber, hubcaps, fishing rods, crescent wrenches. Here, the explanation is simple physics. Loose items are most likely to zing off a vehicle when it is going around a corner.

The very best scenario is one where you have a corner with a bump. That way loose objects are lifted and thrown at the same time. If the corner with a bump happens to be on a busy road, the volume of stuff shooting off can be amazing. An acquaintance of mine, Pierre, has lived off the avails of one such corner for years. Pierre lives in Lac La Hache. His corner is south of Lac La Hache—although exactly where, he won't say. Among the stuff he's found are dozens of sleeping bags, fishing tackle, rifles, tents, two gas barbecues and a set of false teeth that happened to fit his stepdaughter.

Around here, stuff gets added to ditches at a slower pace. Of course, I'm not in it just for the material gain. There is an anthropological interest too. Without seeing a magazine or TV in ten years I could identify cultural trends by what's in the ditch. Not only are there fewer cigarette packages in ditches nowadays, but the packages that do turn up are for Player's Extra Lights, or those menthol things. Drinking patterns have changed too, from Labatt's Blue to Kokanee to Dry beer to Diet Coke.

But I'm getting too scientific. The real joy of ambling around a ditch is the wonder of what people throw away, and why. One loafer? A half-full bottle of Crabtree & Evelyn Milk Bath? A pack of red licorice with only one piece eaten? It gives me something to dwell on until Lily is finished her water project. Then the two of us carry on up the lane to see what kind of junk somebody's stuffed in the mailbox.

Rodent Warrior

Every morning around sunup I go outside to let the chickens out, dump a couple more armloads of firewood by the back door, and check the rat traps in the garage. The traps are at the back, balanced on the rafters. I've got them secured to a length of fish line. That way, when a rat gets caught the trap swings down, like a noose, and prevents the rat from gnawing itself free. Then I give them a whack with a shovel, spring them loose and catapult the carcass down to the beach, for the crabs to do their work.

This isn't the best part of my day. I'm not into trapping rats; I don't even hate them. Put a bushy tail on a rat and you'd have a nice squirrelly-type animal that you'd feed popcorn to and try to pet. What I do hate, though, is the idea of rats. All the stories about them make them out to be so parasitical and gross.

Like the one my friend Robert tells, from the time he worked in a landfill in Port Hardy. At night they'd pit lamp the rats with a spot-light and a .22. There were so many they couldn't miss. Bang, bang, bang. Three rats. But no matter how many they shot, there were always more. And do you know what the live rats did with the dead ones? Dragged them away, just like they would a tossed-out turkey sandwich. Filthy buggers.

And how about the stories of vicious rats. They're so mean they'll actually attack you if cornered. That's why city workers in London had to shoot a twenty-two-pound rat. That's right. Twenty-two pounds. They said they were afraid of it.

In my experience, most rats are harmless. That is, excepting the one or ones that peed in the car last winter. Up to that time we'd heard the intermittent tick of a rat turd in the attic, but didn't give it a thought as they weren't able to get in the actual house. Then it got cold. Soon after, I noticed a sour smell coming out of the car heater. I investi-gated, and discovered a nest by the window-washing fluid. They were climbing in there to get warm and, I guess, peeing. When we'd drive the car the pee would cook. My good going-out sweater still stinks of eau de rodent.

Obviously this wasn't OK. The landlord recommended rat poi-son, but I refuse to have anything to do with the stuff. I used rat poison once, and the rat died in a suitcase. I discovered this two months later, when pulling the suitcase out of a cupboard in preparation for a trip to Calgary. Up popped this half-composted rat. "*Aauugghhh!*" I said. I heaved the suitcase and haven't been off the island since.

That left cats or traps. We wanted a cat anyway, so we went to the feed store, where they had barn kittens for five dollars. We picked a frisky one, believing frisky would lead to vicious. And a female, hearing they're the real killers. (Males get lazy.) Within months, Luba was killing. Hummingbirds. Right out of the air.

Eventually, Luba got a rat. When she brought it into the kitchen we celebrated and said, "Good puss-puss!" and all that, but it didn't do any good. Something about rats put her off. We even tried starving her to hunt, but she simply made up for it by snacking on dozens of tiny shrews instead. Now, when she hears the tick of rat turds on the ceiling, she makes a little motion, looking sideways at us as if to say, "See, can't get it. Ah well, back to the couch."

So that left traps—which is where I am today. The theories about baiting rat traps change all the time. Years ago, there was cheese. Then cheese and jam, ham, ham and cheese, dried dog food, peanut butter, dog food and peanut butter. We've tried Luba's kitty vitamins. The latest fad is peanut butter smeared over bacon, with just a dusting of confectioner's sugar.

My own theory is that you score one rat per new recipe. Then word gets around and you need to revamp the menu, the proof of a satisfied customer being one less tick from the attic when the cold weather comes.

SOLD AT AUCTION

When you live in the country, everyone thinks you have lots of time and lots of space. Within two hundred feet of my back door there is an eclectic inventory that includes three and a half cars, three trucks (one of which has ferns growing off the hood), several portable buildings, a stove without a door, ships' masts, trailers made out of pickup trucks and—this is the most recent addition—four metal desks.

The metal desks are mine. They used to belong to my cousin Steve. He got them last month at the big auction at the Yarrows Shipyard, in Esquimalt. He had gone to the auction intending to buy tools, but had been blindsided by a good deal on desks. Fifteen of them, all resembling Studebakers, for one hundred dollars.

"What are you going to do with fifteen desks?" I asked when he phoned from his home in Cowichan to see if I'd give him a hand muscling them off the site. "I don't know," he fumbled. "It was such a good deal."

This is the type of thing that happens when people from the country go to auctions for anything other than pigs and Charlete cattle. They go in sensible, drain-your-taps-before-winter, cut-your-firewood-in-the-spring folk, and come out with fifteen metal desks.

Or, as in the case of my brother Guy, who went to the same Yarrows auction, they come out with seven drafting tables. Guy knows as much about drafting as a dog knows about its father. But the temptation was too much. One hundred and fifty dollars, seven tables.

The worst case of auction fever I've seen was a friend named Dean. When a Lake Cowichan sawmill closed down in the early 1980s, Dean bought a large quantity of circa 1920s machinery. His thinking, if I can use the word "thinking" in these circumstances, was that he would rebuild the mill, operate it in his spare time, and thus make the transition from lowly electrician to independently wealthy lumber merchant. The machinery was trucked to his yard in Chemainus, where much of it sits to this day, looking like prehistoric fossils in the Badlands.

But this was long before the desks. The deal Steve and I struck when he called was that in return for my labour grunting the desks out, he'd give me a three-drawer all-metal filing cabinet. He didn't have a three-drawer all-metal filing cabinet, but I didn't discover that until the day was done. "Funny," remarked Cousin Steve, scratching his head and looking around the office. "I swore there was one here. Ah well, too bad." What he did have was an immense Gilchrist jack, the type handloggers use to hoist full-length trees into the water. He found this in a room adjacent to the one with his desks. The contents of that room hadn't actually been included in the auction lot but, using the sliding scale of possession, Steve declared ownership. Did I want the Gilchrist jack?

I said no. Where I live, on rented land with a magnificent stand of first-growth Douglas fir, a device like that would surely lead to trouble.

He then suggested as payment a drafting table (that wasn't his), a ladder (rickety) and several dozen lunchroom benches (in case you ever have a big, big party). No, I said. No, no and no. I was still holding out for the three-drawer filing cabinet, but only feebly.

During the day, things got turned around so that Steve was explaining how, if I didn't have a filing cabinet, I must therefore have room for a desk. Or maybe six. I'm no sucker, so I settled for taking four.

We had just finished unloading them into the cabin when Lorna came up from our cabin to check on the merchandise. "I thought we were going to get a filing cabinet," she said. "We *need* a filing cabinet," she said, more firmly. I looked at the desks, then at Steve, then at the desks. "Sure," I said, "but these were such a good deal."

/NTO

SEASON

A week ago today, our cat went into heat. This wasn't entirely unexpected, as two months ago we redirected money from our cat-spaying fund into a new six-cubic-foot contractor's wheelbarrow. At that time we hoped the surrounding country was tomcatless, or, if there were any toms, that they were preoccupied.

We now know this country has plenty of toms, and they aren't preoccupied. Since that first night Luba went into heat, they've been slinking around, fracturing our sleep with their yowling and caterwauling.

Two days after Luba went into season, our landlady separated her Hereford cow from last year's calf. The cow, Magic, is due to calve any time now, and it's important she has plenty of milk for the newborn. Not surprisingly, last year's calf, Peanut, doesn't like this arrangement, and has been bawling for its mother day and night. But especially night.

This is what spring is like around here. Layers of sound—grunting on yowling on bawling—all atop the usual croaking and ribetting and *kneedeep, kneedeep* from the pond and forest. The effect is similar to that of a shake roof: one sound overlaps another until the span from dusk to dawn is a solid ceiling of horny, lonely, unsatiated calls.

When we first moved here, this noise was a problem. Lily mistook it for sirens and added her own late-night wails to the cacophony. "I'm afraid of the frogs!" she'd sob. But after a while, and with much patient explanation from her mother and me about the cycles of nature, she was reassured enough to sleep.

Then, three days ago, Canada geese showed up. Two pair. One pair in the pond behind the house, one pair in the bay below the house.

Canada geese are nothing new here. There was that community of geese that moved into our drinking water that time, and another pair that moved in last year—likely one of the current couples. They nested quietly on a grassy islet in the bay. The only time they made a racket was the day an eagle came around and made several passes at the goslings. We cheered the goose family on that day, mainly because we had several predators circling around us at the time, in the form of banks and phone companies, and were sympathetic to their plight.

This year is different. Instead of getting on with nesting, the geese are expelling loud energy trying to drive the other couple out of the country. The no-man's land in this noisy battle is the roof of our house. Starting at about four-thirty in the morning, one pair claims the roof, honking angrily. Then the other pair drives them off with an equal amount of noise. Back and forth it goes, first one couple taking the offensive, then the other—like a good playoff game, and about as noisy.

The honking of geese is not a sound that fits well into dreams, especially when it's ten feet above your head. I discovered this the first morning the geese arrived. I slipped out of bed and stepped outside onto the deck and in a hushed voice said, "Bugger off!" The trick was to get the geese to go and leave Lily and her mother in peaceful slumber. It worked, too, except a southeaster was blowing off the water that day. Southeasters are cold; I sleep nude. By the time I got back inside, I was so *invigorated* sleep was no longer an option. So I made coffee and fidgeted until the sun came up.

Yesterday, same time, the geese were back on the roof. This time I was smart. I pulled on sweat pants and dashed outside. "Pshaw!" I said. Pshaw is the quietest word you can say loudly. It worked, too— only the geese flew away and Lily got up to see what Dad was doing.

You don't explain anything quickly to a three-year-old, least of all when you're outside half nude saying "Pshaw" to big birds.

"What are you doing?" Lily asked.

"Getting rid of the geese," I mumbled. "Or trying to, anyway."

"But they need to have their eggs," she said, and, with a quivering lip, repeated a version of the nature cycle spiel I'd given her last year. I was going to tell her that the nature cycle isn't the only important event in the world, and that things like the sleep cycle counted too. The nature versus nap lecture. But I heard something that made me change my mind. A small engine, wound out. It was Dave, fetching the newspaper in his Suzuki.

"Plum jam on toast?" I said.

"Sure," Lily bellowed, flapping her arms. "Let's get Mom up!"

ACKNOWLEDGEMENTS

I am indebted to CBC Radio's David Gullason, who first proposed I write a series of essays on country life. His thoughtful suggestions improved these stories immeasurably. I also owe a great deal to Lorna Jackson, for her encouragement, advice and spaghetti sauce.